QHASHEIK'S POD

An Alien Legacy Novella

Keri Kruspe

Cover art by Jacqueline Sweet

Photos created by the help of Midjourney

Edited by ELF

CONTENTS

CHAPTER ONE

"What in the name of *Oxagi* is *that*?"

Qhasheik grimaced at the high note at the end of Coxin's question. Damn, the male screeched so loud, it wouldn't surprise him if his sensitive ears bled. "By the Goddess's titties, boy!" He stuck a knuckle in his ear and wiggled it. "What are you so friggin' excited about?"

He strolled over to the younger male's console. At first, he saw nothing to make the kid so animated. Then, on his floating 3-D monitor, he caught the bizarre image of a planet heading their way.

The orb approached so fast they'd be lucky to avoid smacking into it.

"Evasive maneuvers," Qhasheik shouted. "Now!" He plopped his ass in the command chair and activated its bindings.

Without a word, the other four males on their small bridge scrambled to their stations and strapped in.

The ship's navigator, Todaet, yanked them hard to one side to avoid the barreling sphere.

The planet whizzed by with barely enough room to avoid collision, but the collective sighs in the boxy room were short-lived.

"Oh, shit," Engrox mumbled under his breath.

"Now what?" Qhasheik swiped the chair's bindings away, activated his command monitor, and tied it to the outside visuals. What could the boy be bitching about? He compared his readings to Engrox's, and his heart sank.

A massive shock wave rolled straight for them. When it hit, it might not be as devastating as hitting that planet, but it wouldn't matter. They'd never survive. And it was too late to avoid it.

Time for Plan B. "Head for that fuckin' planet!"

If they made an emergency landing there, the massive thing just might save them.

Todaet's fingers flew across the console as the sharp turn of the ship pressed them all hard into their seats.

"Will we make it?" Qhasheik didn't expect an answer. In fact, he hoped no one gave him one.

Sweat gathered around the base of Todaet's horns. "If I push the engines hard enough..."

"My poor babies. Keep it together, lovely, lovely *Phytro*. Keep it together." Khers gripped the chair's armrest as he prayed to the ship. The centrifugal force was so strong, his head flattened against the chair's back. His eyes squeezed shut. "Dammit, Todaet! You're going to burn her out for sure."

"Better her than us!" Coxin's eggplant-colored skin paled as he smacked a hand over his mouth.

Qhasheik couldn't blame the young one for being nauseous. The forces needed to catch up to the rogue planet were brutal. "Where the fuck is that thing coming from?" he asked through gritted teeth. The only thing big enough from those headings to make that kind of disturbance was...

"Peinuewei."

The defeat in Todaet's voice created a huge knot in Qhasheik's stomach.

Coxin straightened. "What do you mean, Peinuewei? Are you saying our planet got hit by that shock wave?" His horizontal pupils expanded, leaving the thin red ring of his irises barely visible in a sea of black.

Todeat shook his head. "No." His lips pressed into a thin slit. "I'm saying that's what caused the wave." He turned pain-filled eyes to look at Qhasheik. "Our home, Peinuewei, is gone. Destroyed, like something blew it up."

"What?" Coxin pushed on the armrests as if to get out of his seat.

Qhasheik locked the bindings on the boy's chair to keep him safe.

"What do you mean, destroyed?" Large silver tears gathered in Coxin's rapidly blinking eyes. "What do you mean?" His voice raised as he struggled in his chair. "Let me go! I have to go home! My family! I have to see my family!"

He pushed so hard against the restraints, Qhasheik gave a nod to Khers, who doubled as the ship's med-tech as well as the engineer.

Without a word, Khers pulled a hypo-syringe from the medical pouch around his belt. He released his bindings and leaned forward to jab Coxin on the back of his neck.

The boy gasped. Then his eyes rolled up, and he passed out.

"Poor bastard." Engrox's full mouth thinned. "At least if we don't make it, he'll never know."

"What do you think, Todeat? Do you think landing there will give us a chance?" Qhasheik asked.

Toadet shrugged. "I know we'll make it to the planet. But we're coming in so fast, I doubt I can control the landing."

Death by getting demolished in space? Or death by burning up in that planet's atmosphere? Choices... choices. Qhasheik gripped the armrests to see which the All Goddess dished out to them.

"Here! This one's alive."

It was hard to understand the words at first.

The universal translator all Ibbins wore since childhood was having a hard time making sense of the foreign language spoken in alien tones around him.

Qhasheik shook his scrambled brain as he tried to make sense of what was going on.

"Ugly bastard, isn't he?"

Well, that nasty comment was easy enough to understand. Stupid ass couldn't be talking about him, now could he? Slices of agony squeezed Qhasheik's head and raced through him. Why did everything hurt? He swore even his toenails throbbed in pain. He tried to raise his arm to rub his eyes, but his muscles spasmed so hard it wasn't worth the attempt.

It was a struggle, but he found the strength to open his eyes. Surrounded in twilight, the stars above cheerfully twinkled. It wasn't until he sneezed that the stench of seared metal mixed with the unbelievable reek of burned flesh made his nose wrinkle. He sat up with a groan.

Memories flooded, chased by a pain so profound he fought to keep the acidic nausea down. Blinking blurry eyes, Qhasheik leaned back on his elbows. There, in the distance, was his mangled ship. How in the hell did he get thrown out of it? He wouldn't find the answer lying around on his ass. He rolled to stand, but the blunt end of a long laser spear shoved him back down.

"Stay down, you disgusting *gigim xul*."

Who the fuck did this asshole think he was calling an evil spirit? Qhasheik peered up. Standing in front of him was one of the whitest humanoid species he'd ever seen. Skin, hair, even his ridiculous tunic and pants were an alabaster white. The only other color on the guy were his blue-green eyes that matched the rolling glitter in the tip of his laser spear. Several movements behind the guy meant there was more than one bozo lurking around. Of course there was. Why wouldn't there be?

"Where's my crew?" He glanced at his burning ship in the distance. "We've got to get my men!" Taking a deep breath, tried once again to stand.

And once again, the ghost-man pushed them back. "I told you to stay down. Dudu, get a *Nutesh* snare on this piece of yetu.

Dudu? Yetu? Qhasheik swallowed a snicker. Choice. The man ordered a guy named Dudu to get something after he'd called him a piece of shit.

Rough hands grabbed him under his arms and pulled him up.

"Hey, not so rough! I was trying to get up, but this jerk kept pushing me back." He shrugged to get out of their grip. No such luck. Between one breath and the next, something hard and cold snapped around his neck. Piercing needles embedded themselves in his skin.

They weren't long enough to cause serious injury but sharp enough to keep the collar in place.

The two white aliens who held him in a punishing grip shoved him away. He stumbled, but righted before he ended up face-first on the teal-colored grass. Gripping the edges of the tight neck brace, he tried to pull it off. All he got for his efforts were stabbing pains as the sharp needles burrowed deeper.

"I wouldn't do that if I were you." The first guy chuckled. "The *Nutesh* snare is your new best friend. Here, let me show you." He aimed a tiny black box in Qhasheik's direction and pushed the yellow button on top.

Instant agony obliterated all thought and body functions. Qhasheik screamed and flopped to the ground in an undignified heap, twitching and squirming with no control. The pain stopped as abruptly as it started. Taking a fortifying breath, he gazed back at the canopy of stars overhead, twinkling in mockery. They taunted him, announcing his cherished freedom was long gone.

The homely mug of the first alien blocked his celestial view. "Got it, *shep-sin*? You're all mine now."

Qhasheik ignored the guy's claim he'd boned Qhasheik's mother. "What about my crew? Are they all right? Where are they?"

"Pick him up."

The sight of the distant stars slid away as Qhasheik was once again yanked to his unsteady feet. "My crew." He tried to ask again.

"Oh, I wouldn't worry about those other freaks." The male's cold eyes narrowed in an up-and-down perusal. His fat lips curled at one corner. "Trust me, they're all dead. Torn to pieces and burned to a nice, toasty crisp."

Everything around Qhasheik darkened. "Dead? All four of them? Are you sure?"

The male snorted. "Yeah, trust me. We checked that wreck twice. You're the only one who survived. And we almost missed finding you. Ain't it lucky we did?" The alabaster male let loose an evil chuckle that made his bulbous belly rock.

A sour taste coated Qhasheik's mouth. "What are you going to do with me?" Shit. Why ask? Doubtful it'd be anything good.

The guy licked his fat lips and stared at Qhasheik's crotch. "After I've enjoyed you every way I can think of, I'll sell you at the slave market." He rubbed his hands together.

"Welcome to Akurn."

CHAPTER TWO

"I can't believe how busy we've been. Boy, am I ever glad you talked me into doing this. Getting away was just what we needed."

Katsuki grinned. Her heart swelled at Arzea's admission. It'd taken some serious parental nagging. Okay, a shitload of nagging sprinkled with a heaping dose of guilt to pull her daughter away from her classes at the university.

Even though it was break time at school, Arzea planned on staying there to attend extracurricular classes. Just as she'd done two years in a row.

Katsuki might be proud of her daughter's devotion to her studies, but enough was enough. All too soon, Arzea would graduate and leave home for good. Taking this vacation was the best thing they could've done to spend uninterrupted time together before that happened.

"Don't tell me you're admitting you had fun." When Arzea nodded, Katsuki snickered. "Yeah? Then by the Lady of All Life, I'd better alert the media."

Arzea leaned back in her co-pilot chair with her hands clasped behind her head. Her dreamy smile spoke volumes. "Jeez, *Sia*."

Mother, Arzea called her mother. How long had it been since her adult child called Katsuki that?

"What's not to love? The pleasure planet of Agnon had everything. Sun, fun, and a virtual smorgasbord of gorgeous males to choose from. I swear, I need a vacation from my vacation."

Katsuki's smile widened in agreement. While the two of them stayed at the same hotel, they kept different rooms so they could enjoy in private the sensual delights Agnon offered.

The only downside was that the resort was a couple of systems away from Runihura.

The journey of five solar days to get there and back was a bonus, giving her quiet time with Arzea. Plus, she had fun flexing her unused piloting skills, getting there and back in the top-of-the-line personal star ship she'd recently purchased. Running Narkata, the small moon orbiting their home world, left little free time. It shouldn't surprise her Arzea had a tendency to be a workaholic like her mother.

"I know what you mean." Katsuki admitted. "I'm afraid I won't be taking any more time off in the foreseeable future. No telling what a mess Eiael left the place."

When Arzea agreed at the last minute to go away with her, she'd scrambled to find somebody to take over the running of the vast estate as well as oversee the mining operations that made their House so profitable. Out of sheer desperation, she asked her cousin to run things on Narkata while she was away.

While Eiale might be smart enough to run the place short term, her greedy disposition worried Katsuki. Thank the Lady of All Life her cousin wouldn't be there long enough to cause a riot among the workers.

Just her luck, her estate manager had to go to Runihura to take care of her ailing mother. And finding a replacement was turning out to be a real pain in the ass. Katsuki threw her shoulders back. First thing on her agenda, find a new overseer. No more dickin' around.

She glanced at her daughter who was sitting back with her eyes closed and her mouth relaxed in sleep. She'd always hoped Arzea would take over the family business. But her daughter's obsession with alien studies was as far from running Narkata as she could get.

The ship gave a small shudder.

What the hell? Katsuki studied the ship's monitors. Nothing should cause that kind of disturbance in the sleek vastness of open space.

"Computer, analyze interior systems. What caused the ship to shake like that?"

"Acknowledged." The metallic monotone voice of the ship responded.

"What's the matter?" Arzea rubbed her pupilless neon-green eyes and sat up. She looked around, her gaze dull with sleep.

"I don't…"

"Analyzation complete." The computer interrupted. "Major engine failure. I have initiated contingency protocol by activating an emergency beacon. It is advisable that all personnel secure themselves in their seats."

"Make sure you're strapped in, honey," Katsuki told her daughter. With a critical eye, she studied the diagnostics displayed on the navigation monitor. How in the hell did the main fuel line fall apart like that? Especially here. The nearest star system was thousands of parsecs away. If they ended up stranded in this uninhibited part of the galaxy, they wouldn't have enough power for food or air until someone responded to their call.

"Computer, analyze what caused the fuel line to disintegrate like that."

Before they left, she had her head mechanic go over every inch of the ship. That part of the ship should've been one of the first things she checked. Damn, that fuel line didn't just get loose. The material itself had dissolved as if bathed in some type of acid. She waved open the chair's security bands to head to the lower levels where the engine room was.

"There is an incoming response to the emergency beacon." The metallic voice of the computer said. "Display?"

Katsuki was about to step out of the bridge. Someone was near enough to help?

"What? Yes. Yes! Put it on the main viewer." She rushed back to her seat and clicked on the outside viewers. Headed their way was something so astounding her mouth dropped open.

Arzea's delicate brow furrowed. "What's that? Is that... is that a rogue planet?"

"I think you're right." Katsuki studied the sphere. "Didn't you once tell me it's estimated there are billions of them roaming the galaxy, none bound to any star or brown dwarf? I never imagined I'd see one in my lifetime. Computer—" She leaned forward to review the readouts. "—quick analyzation of the approaching planet."

"It's a Class Six planet with a circumference of around 45,000 standard star leagues."

Oh, good. Class Six meant it had a breathable atmosphere.

"It hosts an advanced civilization with just under a billion sentient beings."

"Magnify it on the main view screen." Katsuki ordered.

What the computer didn't tell her was the beauty of the approaching globe. Swirls of reds, yellows, and browns mixed under an overlay of gray and black coating the sky. Must be some type of shield to keep their atmosphere in. Twinkling lights around it made it appear to be in perpetual twilight.

"Unidentified craft. Identify yourself."

Katsuki jeered at the guttural male baritone of the voice coming out of the ship's speakers. She glanced at her daughter with a knowing smirk. Looks like they had to deal with males on this planet.

"You're hailing the *StarSong* from Narkata." No need to claim they were from Runihura until they knew who they were dealing with. From childhood it was drilled into them to protect their homeworld at all costs. "We are suffering from engine failure. Are you able to assist?"

"Affirmative. Power down and we will send a magnetism beam to guide you."

She shivered. She hated relying on unknown species. A sense of foreboding crept in. But what choice did they have? Either take a chance with these people or die a horrible space-induced death.

"Mom—" Arzea grabbed Katsuki's hand. "—I have a bad feeling about this."

"I do too, my love." She squeezed back. "I do too."

"Stop. Do not come any farther. We demand to speak to the male in charge!"

Katsuki put herself in front of Arzea as they walked down the open plank from their ship to the inner hanger after the magnetism tractor beam disconnected. With narrowed eyes, she studied the strange looking humanoid aliens that made a show of surrounding them. Three in front, another three by an open door, and, if she wasn't mistaken, there were at least two on each side behind them. Nothing she couldn't handle.

"Male in charge?" She crossed her arms, widened her stance, and studied the alabaster-skinned aliens. While they weren't as marble-white as the people from her home planet, these beings bore a slight translucent tinge of silver. And nary a female in sight. She frowned. She could understand having males in the guard detail because they were physically stronger than females, but it was a well-known fact that males didn't have the brain capacity or emotional stability to make strategic decisions. Look at them, each one squatting with scowls and raised spear-like weapons. Quivering as if they barely controlled themselves. She doubted any of them had two brain cells to rub together.

"Females." He snorted and gave his companions next to him an ugly sneer. "You are obviously so stupid you don't know what being in charge means." His companions chuckled with him. "Now be a good little female and get me your master. I'll be damned if I waste my time speaking to a female." The guy growled.

The asshole actually growled. Like that was supposed to scare her enough to make her jump to his bidding.

He sauntered close and pointed his spear up, thumping the blunt end on the metallic floor. "Get him now!"

The alien male tromped near, giving her a chance to analyze him better.

The strange pigmentation of his nearly colorless skin contrasted with the copper-colored breastplate that matched the metallic wrist- and armbands on his naked arms. His matching conical helmet covered both ears and the back of his thick neck. Covering his bulky torso was a short-sleeved, one-piece tunic of indigo and quasar blue, held in place by an animal-skin belt with flowing tassels at the ends. Billowing pantaloons were tucked into knee-high boots of the same material as his belt.

But it was his eyes, his strange foreign eyes, that made her breath catch.

Instead of the single, clear, neon colors her people sported, his had a dimensional trait. The background was white as a blizzard during the cold season. In the middle was a round orb, with a black center surrounded by a broad band of sapphire blue. As his gaze roamed over her body, the inner black expanded, practically obliterating the blue color. He licked his floppy lips, exposing his stained, crooked teeth. A snowflake-white rectangular chin beard reached the middle of his throat, littered with fresh crumbs from a recent meal.

"Well—" She sidestepped to block Arzea further. "—we're all there is. So you only have me to deal with, bub."

The male drew back. His platinum eyebrows rose. "Sacrilege! Uncovered females, even lowly alien ones, may not show themselves in public without a male escort." He crouched and pointed his spear with the swirling cerulean blue tip mere inches from her throat. Without taking his bizarre eyes from her, he spoke out the side of his mouth. "Put a *Nutesh* snare on these disgusting *lilits*.

Oh, no. That asshole did not call her and her daughter whores. Katsuki backhanded the spear away. "I don't know what you think you're..."

Something sharp and stiff cut her words off when it clicked around her neck. Razor-edge needles pierced her skin. Gasping, she tried to pull it off, but the males jerked her hands behind her as a cold metallic band snapped her wrists together. At Arzea's sharp cry, Katsuki sprang into action. Countless hours of training took over. She kicked the jerk behind her and spun around to do the same to the clueless moron in front of her.

Both males landed with hard thuds on the ground.

With quick efficiency, she looped her arms under her butt and jumped to put her hands in front of her. Grabbing the fusion phase blaster she had hidden strapped to her hip, she stun-blasted a guard rushing at her. The satisfying beam pulsated and hit the guy in the middle of his chest.

Arms and legs flew wide as he bounced hard on his ass.

"*Sia*! Behind you!"

Responding to Arzea's cry, she shot another alabaster male as he tried to sneak up on her mere clicks behind her.

He fell face-first on the unyielding floor.

She inhaled the satisfying metallic heat that rose off the pistol. At the sound of her daughter struggling, she sprinted in her direction. Only to be stopped as white-hot pain surged through her. Her blaster flew out of her hand, and she crashed to her knees. Searing agony took over, destroying higher thought and motor skills. She thumped hard onto her side, her eyes wide and unblinking. The pain left as the echoing sound of Arzea's scream in the background made her heart race. Dusty, scuffed brown boots filled her sight.

"Not so mighty now, are ya, you fucking bitch!"

The cackling laughter from the chief guard made her wince inside as he towered over her. A click came before another engulfing wave of torture took over. The agony radiating from the foreign collar intensified, making her jerk uncontrollably.

One day, asshole. One. Day.

His scornful guffaw was the last thing she heard before darkness took over.

CHAPTER THREE

A biditan loved his elder brother, Warad-Mushtal. No, really he did. But if the man opened his yap one more time, he'd rearrange the guy's pretty pearlies with his fist. "I'm leaving, and that's all there's to it." He sliced his hand through the air. "I know you mean well, but this is something I have to do. And it's non-negotiable." He tossed in a scowl to show he meant business.

"No, it isn't. You're just being stubborn."

Oh, for the love of the Goddess. There the man stood, fists on hips and tapping a foot like he had a say in anything Abiditan did. Well, technically, he had the right, as the eldest son of their father, Warlord Mattaki-Bunu. One day, his brother would have absolute say in what happened to everyone in their noble house. But today wasn't that day.

Warad-Mushtal lowered his head and gave him a narrow-eyed glare. "Besides, it'll kill Mother if her baby disappears for another rotation in this Goddess-forsaken solar system."

Abiditan couldn't help it. He rolled his eyes. "Oh, for fuck's sake. Put away the Mother guilt card." He mirrored his brother's stance, tapping foot and all. "There's nothing you can do or say to change my mind. You know as well as I do that if I stayed here, I could never leave Esharra for the rest of my life. Not with that warrant out for my arrest and all." Living at the vast estate might not be a hardship, especially since the alternative was being incarcerated at the atrocious maximum-security prison Erset La Tari. *Heh.* That is, if he didn't get executed first.

Well, that's what he got for being born with a deformity that made him an outcast. While he might look like an average Akurn from a distance, once you got close enough, it was clear there was something different about him. His eyes. His Goddess-damned eyes. Instead of the wide variety of shades of blue most Akurns had, his were a mismatch of colors. The right eye was a normal sea-blue green, while his left eye sported a translucent metallic gray.

Warad-Mushtal dropped his hands and engulfed Abiditan in a tight hug, hard enough he couldn't breathe. He returned the hug with his eyes closed. The one thing he never doubted was his family's love for him.

"I'd kill anyone who tried to take you." Warad-Mushtal's words were muffled in Abiditan's hair before he pulled back. Framing his brother's face with his large palms, Warad-Mushtal gave him a steady stare. "King Du-Uru would rue the day he crossed us."

Abiditan covered his brother's hands with his. "I know. But don't you see? That's why I have to go. Me staying here just puts everybody in danger. If I go with Damuzi, Kud, and Edinni to create a hidden city on the Earth's moon, I'll finally be of use to someone instead of a burden." He stepped out of his brother's hold. "Besides, with all the other misfits there, maybe I'll find the love of my life." His heart raced at the thought. He had no trouble leaving Akurn behind. If he stayed here, he'd live looking over his shoulder all the time to avoid getting arrested. Besides, starting over on a new world might give him a chance to find someone to share his life with. Or at the very least, be with people who looked at him with anything besides disgust.

"Ha! There's the real reason right there."

Warad-Mushtal slapped a meaty palm on his back, making Abiditan stumble. Damn man must hit the training grounds more than usual. He shrugged and rubbed his shoulder to get rid of the sharp sting.

"I hope you've discussed this with Mother and Father before telling me." Warad-Mushtal tilted his head, his steely turquoise gaze unwavering. When Abiditan didn't answer, he stepped back. "At least tell me you told Homa about this."

Abiditan pressed his lips together. He'd rather jump off the nearest cliff before confessing his plans to his sister and parents. Isn't that what a big brother was for? Besides, he had a holo-vid explaining where he was going and why. All Warad-Mushtal had to do was play it for the family after Abiditan left. That way, he'd avoid all the emotional crap and leave with a clear conscience. The last thing he needed was to be confused about his purpose.

"No, there isn't time." He pressed the vid-disc into his brother's hand. "Here's all you need to know about where I'm going and what I'm doing. Once you show it to the family, make sure you erase it and any information that might have seeped into the system. I'm sure you know the monarchy inspects everyone's systems. We can't afford for them to suspect the family of anything."

"But..."

"To make this even better, I've made a separate file showing my fake death at our abum's hand." Having his father execute him would prove the rest of the family were staunch patriots to the royal family. "That way, the authorities won't come here looking for me. Best of all, it will advance father's position in King Du-Uru's inner circle. It'll give us more power and protection."

"You..."

Abiditan grabbed his brother in a last hug. He squeezed and pulled back, blinking away the gathering tears. "Once I leave through the Transkip in my room, destroy it. I'll send you a message once I arrive at FarDeep base to let you know I made it."

Warad-Mushtal sucked in a breath with a hiss. "I don't like this one bit."

The sorrow in his eyes told Abiditan his brother realized this was a good option for all of them. "Don't worry, Brother. I'll only be gone one rotation around the sun." He gave a forced chuckle. "Who knows? Maybe by then, our xenophobic society will come out of the dark ages and embrace those of us who are different."

Warad-Mushtal snorted. "Little brother, you've always had a vivid imagination."

CHAPTER FOUR

Bending to study the schematic printout of the unfamiliar room he was in, Abiditan concentrated on the layouts for the family units he was in charge of. An enticing scent made his nose twitch. Goosebumps slid along the back of his neck, and his heart raced.

Without looking around, he sensed the strange alien had to be around somewhere. Watching him. Again. Tilting his head to take a peek out of the corner of his eye, the splash of dusky, dark purple confirmed his suspicions.

Annoyance warred with excitement. The first time he'd first seen the strange-looking creature, he'd been so surprised he stared at the guy like an immature child. Standing there with his mouth open like an idiot who hadn't seen an alien before. Which wasn't true. The ruling class of Akurn had inundated their homes with various alien species from the planets they'd invaded and pillaged throughout the galaxy for eons.

But this one... just by his mere presence, he held Abiditan spellbound. It wasn't the darkened skin color so different from his. And it wasn't the set of thick, black horns curling at the side of the alien's head, with the gray hairless limb running between them. Nor were those cherry-red eyes with the horizontal black pupil what caught his attention. While the male's mouth-watering, tight physique was something out of a badly written erotic novel, that's not what made his breath catch.

It was the way the male gave Abiditan his undivided attention. That intense gaze would roam over him as it explored every inch before settling back with pupils dilated, full of suggestion.

Abiditan swore he felt every visual caress, as if the male stroked him with his hands. All it took was having the creature in the same room with him, and all intelligent speech went bye-bye. Higher thought fled as his blood headed south. His damn traitorous dick twitched and filled with anticipation. The only thing he could do to keep his sanity was to run away like a coward every chance he got.

Lately, that was getting harder to do. The male seemed to be everywhere, watching him from a distance. In the next room, or just down the street. It happened so often, other Akurns began to harass the shit out of him.

He had a hard enough time working with the prejudiced population as it was. He didn't need this bullshit to make things harder for him. While his family's name carried some clout, working as a laborer putting together the moon city with the other outcasts didn't give him any slack. In fact, the only difference between working here and on Akurn was that here they weren't threatening to arrest or execute him for being different.

But why push it? Throwing his shoulders back, with sure strides he headed to the alien male. The... what in the hell was his species called again? Oh, that's right, Ibbin. He shoved away the memories of searching the computer database about the guy after the first time he'd seen him.

The Ibbin stood from the crouch he'd been in as he rolled a rope in a tight circle around his shoulder and bent elbow. With each motion, his bulky arms bunched and released. The male had taken off his loose tunic in the blazing heat of the room, exposing the hills and valleys of his muscular chest, free of male nipples. In the low light, the richness of his dark skin reflected in an iridescent sheen of perspiration.

Abiditan's mouth dried. "You, there." He pointed a finger so the guy wouldn't have any doubt he was talking to him. "What are you doing? Don't you have some other place you're supposed to be?" He had every right to ask. It was a reasonable question since the alien wasn't part of his work detail.

The Ibbin's bright-red eyes widened. The corners of his full lips were a captivating blend of black and purple that slid into an alluring smile. When his lips parted, it exposed a hint of upper and lower fangs. With slow, sensual strides, the male faced him.

"Oh, hell no. I'm right where I'm supposed to be—" He licked his bottom lip and glanced at Abiditan's crotch before looking him straight in the eye. "—Abiditan."

Abiditan stilled. "How do you know my name?"

The male shrugged, and his smile widened. "I've done everything I could to learn about you."

Abiditan glanced around. Good, the place was empty. The last thing he needed was someone overhearing that dumbass statement. Heat ran up his neck and filled his face. "I don't think..."

Before he got another word in, the Ibbin was mere inches from him. Close enough, his body heat wrapped around Abiditan like a warm blanket.

"Don't think. Feel." Even closer. "We belong together." He reached out and caressed Abiditan's cheek. "I know you feel it too." Any space between their bodies was long gone. Chest to chest, groin to groin.

The hard thickness of the male's arousal pushed against Abiditan's lower belly.

"I have to taste you." The alien's breath fanned his face as he stared at Abiditan's mouth, then slid his hands slid around the back of his captive's neck as if to make sure he didn't move.

Abiditan's lips parted in anticipation.

The Ibbin didn't hesitate, accepting the invitation. His semi-rough black tongue slid over Abiditan's, enticing him to taste back.

The male's flavor was a crazy mixture of primeval virility and wild intoxicating spice. Abiditan moaned and sucked on the rough flesh as the heat of the kiss seared the back of his throat. An electric stream of lust traveled down his spine and pooled at his groin, making him hard with need. He couldn't think past his eagerness as the Ibbin claimed him with absolute authority.

A shattering bang in another room jerked them apart.

Befuddled, the only thing Abiditan could do was stand there with his mouth open.

"When does your shift end?" the Ibbin whispered. His hands were clenched hard enough at his side that his knuckles turned a light violet.

"What?" Abiditan backed away. "No." And like the coward he was, he ran out of the room as fast as he could.

Shit. He didn't even ask for the guy's name.

With mixed feelings Qhasheik watched the Akurn run away. That kiss left no doubt the male was as attracted to him as he suspected. But the guy running away meant he had a lot of hard work ahead of him. He smacked his lips, savoring the male's taste. Damn, what fun he'll have exploring the wild passion between them. He suspected it'd end up a lifelong adventure. Now, wouldn't that be glorious? After that kiss, there was no doubt they shared the soul-pull. Good thing he was a patient male.

Yeah, well... sort of.

CHAPTER FIVE

Qhasheik found extra duties to keep him near Abiditan from then on.

It'd only been a couple of weeks since he'd first laid eyes on Abiditan by accident. When he'd come into the private housing unit, angry voices caught his attention. Hoping it wasn't a fellow alien suffering at the hands of some narrow-minded Akurn, he treaded with light steps and approached the walled-off room. There he spied a male Akurn being berated by a shorter, older Akurn, who was waving a finger in the younger male's face.

Abiditan pushed the finger away and placed his fists on his hips. Whatever that old fart wanted him to do, Abiditan wasn't having any part of it. The rotund male continued to argue in a tone of disgust, treating the other as if he was beneath him. All the younger male did was stand there with a blank face, no reaction to whatever the asshole bitched about.

The old guy stomped a foot and threw his hands up when Abiditan didn't answer. With a harsh "Bah!" the portly elder stomped out of the room. When he passed Qhasheik, the pudgy bastard shoved him on his shoulder as if he was in the way. "Abominations, and now a disgusting alien. This place is full of evil *idimmus*!"

Gods, Qhasheik loved it when other species called him a demon. That moniker had his name written all over it.

"We're all doomed! Goddess, save us all."

Qhasheik winced at the parting high-pitched whine from the bastard that stung his ears. Good thing the annoying shit left.

He savored his taste of semi-freedom here on FarDeep base, but he wasn't stupid enough to go around bitch-slapping all the assholes that irritated him. That would end up a full-time job. He sighed, watching the portly fellow waddle away. Some days, it wasn't worth the headache. No matter how happy it'd make him.

The sound of construction made him curious. Taking a careful peek around the doorjamb to make sure he wasn't seen. Qhasheik got a good look at the younger Akurn. There he was, directing a sealing droid to work on putting up a wall.

As proud as any fictional god, he'd whipped off his top tunic, exposing a magnificent chest slick with perspiration.

Qhasheik licked his lips as his gaze slid over the bright Akurn skin, tracing the carved expanse of the male's tight chest and the rumbling terrain of his abdomen. All that delicious scenery made him stand there like an idiot with his mouth open. The urge to savor all that smooth, succulent skin with his tongue threatened to override elusive common sense.

It wasn't until the Akurn whipped around as if sensing Qhasheik behind the wall that he realized he wasn't supposed to be there. Not taking a chance of getting discovered, he rushed out of the place.

Walking blindly through the various building sites, he contemplated what had just happened. One thing was for sure, the instant attraction that slammed into him couldn't, shouldn't, be ignored.

There was an Ibbin legend of a soul-pull that happened when two people who'd been true loves in a previous life met in this one.

Qhasheik always thought that romantic stuff was a load of crap, but one look at the breathtaking Akurn changed his mind. From now on, he'd learn as much as possible about the male before introducing himself.

Over the next few days, he discovered the other Akurns treated Abiditan as much of an outcast as Qhasheik was. The more he learned about the guy, the harder it was to understand why others treated him like an untouchable.

It wasn't until he overheard two Akurns talking about Abiditan's eyes did it dawn on him what their problem was. Like two different eye colors made him less than them. Ridiculous motherfuckers. All they had to do was take their heads out of their asses and look into those intelligent eyes. There, his nobility and dignity shone through.

What confused Qhasheik was how the guy took the abuse, no matter how roughly they treated him. That humbling fact made him pause. He'd have to be smooth with this one. It wouldn't do any good to push the guy into any type of relationship with him. Yeah, best to take his time. Nice and easy like.

To start his campaign, he volunteered for any menial task that put him around Abiditan. He made sure he never got too close and personal. That way, the guy would get used to seeing him as he wormed his way into the other man's consciousness.

He couldn't wait to show the male that he deserved to be cherished and loved—just the way he was.

When enough time passed, he approached his love to make his motives clear.

Qhasheik didn't intend to kiss the Akurn when they first spoke. But when those mismatched eyes darkened in interest, who was he to resist? That kiss turned out way better than he'd hoped. By the All Goddess, Abiditan's voice was a sultry baritone that made him shiver with anticipation. When those blazing orbs focused on him, he flung his shoulders back, savoring the sensation when he'd examined the male from head to toe.

And that kiss. It shot to hell any other experience Qhasheik'd ever had. With a shudder, he relived tasting and feeling all that glorious body against his. And there was no mistaking the hard evidence Abiditan sported when they embraced.

The Akurn wasn't as disinterested as he liked others to think. Qhasheik didn't miss Abiditan's nervous glances whenever they ended up in the same room with others. As if he wanted to make sure no one else discovered their mutual attraction. Maybe the male was protecting himself, but all too soon it also became clear he wanted to protect Qhasheik from suffering when he boldly looked at any Akurn.

Damn, that realization made him harder than ever. Not that his freaking dick listened to him. Stupid thing had a mind of its own. No matter how often he relieved the ache at night with his own hand, it didn't help. All it took was one look at Abiditan and it erected at full attention like a good little soldier.

Well, if everything went as planned, tonight his cock would get what it strained for—a close, personal introduction to some glorious Abiditan flesh.

CHAPTER SIX

A biditan zoned out, ignoring the sounds and various aromas in the makeshift tavern. Why he came here was anyone's guess. The last thing he wanted was to get drunk or find some slob who wanted a pity lay.

So far, neither option was on the horizon.

He gripped the tumbler containing the same drink he ordered hours ago. No one approached him for conversation or anything else. He slumped on a barstool until a wild, free scent made him straighten, his heart racing. Even through the boisterous chaos, he sensed the minute the Ibbin entered the room.

He tightened his hold on his glass, keeping his back facing the open door. Glancing at the mirror behind the bar, he watched the purple-skinned alien wend his way through the crowded room, making a beeline straight for him.

Abiditan broke out in a sweat. Coming toward him was the male who haunted his memories and dreams. He squirmed on the hard seat as his dick filled the closer the male came.

Damn, he hated the way his body responded around the dark-skinned alien. And him wearing that close-fitting, one-piece employee's work suit that lovingly clung to his body didn't help. He glanced around the room. Damn, no chance to escape quietly through this crowd.

He jerked his head to keep an eye on the alien and got caught in the male's otherworldly gaze on the mirror. Everything around him fell away as he stared into the promising heat in the Ibbin's eyes.

A murmur of laughter and condescending catcalls faded into the background as the Ibbin grabbed the chair next to him and threw a leg over the backless barstool to plop onto the seat. The evocative scent of male musk combined with an alluring tang of an unfamiliar spice filled Abiditan with an inexplicable urge to grab the male and dominate him with his mouth. And he wasn't envisioning a traditional kiss on the mouth. To keep from doing something stupid, he grasped the round tumbler holding the misty alcoholic concoction. He raised it to his lips for a sip, allowing the burning liquid to coat his lips and tongue before he swallowed.

"Can I tempt you for more?"

Fuck, was the Ibbin asking about a drink or another kiss? And double-damn, the guy's smoky voice should be illegal.

Abiditan slammed the thick glass onto the stone-derived counter. Taking a chance, he swung his gaze to the alien. "No, thanks. I was just leaving."

He rose. Now he'd walk away and prove one and for all to the male he wasn't interested.

With a knowing grin, the Ibbin waved for him to sit. "Don't leave, *greica*. I promise not to bite." He leaned in. "Not unless you want me to." His seductive tone was low enough no one else heard the words.

The unbidden image of the Ibbin's sharp fangs tickling across his sensitive cock made Abiditan's knees weak. His ass dropped onto the chair.

"Good boy. Now sit, relax. We'll just have a friendly little chat." The Ibbin raised a forefinger to the Akurn minding the bar. "Another round, if you would, my good man."

The elderly Akurn raided his bushy white eyebrows. "You want what he's havin'?"

The Ibbin glanced at Abiditan's now-empty glass.

The last of the murky red liquor congealed at the bottom. *Qhut* was one of the highest proof liquors on the planet. Most alien species couldn't handle the fiery liquid. It'd serve the pushy male right if it tossed him on his ass after one sip.

"Yeah." Abiditan nodded to the bottle gripped in the aged barkeep's trembling fist. "Let him have it." He turned to the Ibbin with a smirk. "I'm sure our friend here can handle it."

"Okay—" The guy shrugged. "—but when he passes out, it's up to you to clean up the mess and take him outta here." With his other hand, he pulled a clean glass from behind himself and poured a shot into it.

Swirling, misty, red-and-white liquor settled when he put the glass in front of the Ibbin.

His clear unblinking stare never looked the drink.

Instead, his unwavering stare held Abiditan spellbound. He couldn't help but get lost in the male's strange eyes as they focused on him. The unusual black background was a contrasting foil to his red irises with their horizontal black pupils, now dilated.

The end of that gray limb between his horns, resting on his back, lazily flicked. "Here's to you, *greica*." Without taking his eyes off Abiditan, the Ibbin raised his glass and downed the liquor in one gulp.

When the male put the glass on the countertop, Abiditan waited for him to pass out.

Instead of doing the expected, the handsome purple alien rested an elbow on the counter and laid his cheek on his fist. His unusual eyes roamed over Abiditan's body as he wielded a smoldering smile. "Has anyone told you how absolutely breathtaking you are, *greica*?"

It wasn't hard to hear the sincerity in his voice.

Abiditan frowned. "Why do you keep calling me that? What does it mean?"

The Ibbin scooted his barstool closer. "It means gorgeous." He licked his black lips and stared at Abiditan's. "You are definitely that and much, much more."

The tension tightening Abiditan's neck lessened. Now the guy was messing with him. Nobody ever said he was anything other than disgusting. This male had to be looking for a quick lay. That he could handle. It'd been a long time since he'd indulged in mind-blowing sex with anyone. Much less with someone as exotic as this alien.

With a quick, disgusted snort, he leaned in and lessened the distance between them. "No need to spout ridiculous lies. I'm not some female you have to woo. If all you wanted was a quick fuck, all you had to do was say so."

The Ibbin sat back with a frown and contemplated him, stroking his square chin. "You think that's what I'm after?" His frown turned into an evil leer. "You Akurns might be a xenophobic lot in public, but I assure you I can fuck anyone here with a crook of my finger." He waved to the crowded room without looking at them. "If that's all I was looking for. Which it isn't." He fisted his hand on his lap. "And a *quick fuck* isn't what's happening between us, now is it?"

Abiditan hunched his shoulders. "I don't know what in the hell you're talking about." The guy couldn't mean what he thought he did. Could he? The only way he'd ever coaxed someone into his bed was to promise not to tell anyone they'd gotten together. And if he was lucky to have more than a one-night stand, it was an unspoken agreement between the two of them not to acknowledge the fact to the public.

With a tilt to his horned head, the Ibbin pursed his full lips. He pulled the gray limb from his back and rested it over his shoulder. With a soft smile, he stroked the soft-looking skin. "Who has hurt you, Akurn?"

Abiditan jerked away. His hand smacked the half-full tumbler and knocked it off the bar. Good thing it was made of non-breakable material.

It bounced and rolled away on the hard floor, the precious liquid pooling on the floor.

He jumped off the stool and grabbed the glass and slammed it onto the counter, then he turned to the other male. "I don't know what you're talking about. I'm just fine." He stood his ground with his arms crossed. "Look, I think we've gotten off track here. If you want to go someplace private and have a few laughs, okay. But let's not make it into something it isn't."

The avid interest in the Ibbin's eyes made his mouth dry.

The alien glanced around the room before Abiditan became his sole focus again. "I agree. We should take this somewhere private." His lips lifted in a genuine smile. "Your place or mine?"

Abiditan dropped his arms with an inaudible sigh. Yeah, this he could handle. Wait, everyone lived in makeshift barracks. Unless you were a co-founder. Which he was pretty sure the alien wasn't one. He forced a laugh. "I doubt we'll find any privacy in the common quarters."

The Ibbin stood and brought his muscular body within inches.

Abiditan fought the instinct to step back. Too bad his cock didn't get the message it wasn't going to get any attention today. It filled when he inhaled the alien spice that came with the male's warmth.

"Don't worry, my love."

The tempting whisper held him hostage.

"Follow me and I'll take you to paradise."

"A storage shed?" Abiditan couldn't believe where the Ibbin had taken him. "Won't that be, ah, crowded?"

"What, you don't trust me?" Qhasheik laughed. "I'd never take you anywhere so crass."

Abiditan eyed the enforced metal hut no bigger than his closet back at Esharra. In the middle was a crude door outline with a lock panel big enough for a hand print.

"When I first came here, they tried to put me in with the rest of the aliens in a cramped compound."

His derisive snort made Abiditan chuckle.

"Of course, I refused." Qhasheik put his hand on the panel, which glowed as it read his profile. "I told them if they wanted any help with their failing recycling project, they'd better get me a place of my own. And by the Goddess's titties, they couldn't get me this fast enough."

The front panel of the strange colored unit opened.

Abiditan'd never seen a more disagreeable shade of whatever coated the outside in his life. "What in the seven systems is this obnoxious color?"

"Ah, it's one of my favorites. I call it fuchsia. Nice, eh?" He glanced at Abiditan with a wide grin. "No offense, but you Akurns are so boring. If it isn't some shade of blue or green, you ignore the entire color spectrum." He patted the metal frame as he entered. "Besides, the bold statement scares everyone else spitless." With a flourish, he pulled on Abiditan's elbow. "I told you I'd take you to paradise!"

Abiditan did a double take at the interior.

On one side of the rectangular room was a massive bed with fluffy linens of shocking bright orange that took up half the room. On the other side was a small eating unit with a replicator in the middle of the round table. In the corner was a refresher section with the state-of-the-art facility that eliminated waste and cleaned the body at the same time.

Abiditan whistled. The presence of that expensive contraption made him study the alien with fresh eyes. He doubted even the co-founders had their own private setup like this Ibbin did.

The door closed with a click behind him.

"Would you like a drink?" The Ibbin turned around to face the replicator.

One of Abiditan's weakness when taking a lover was intelligence. Nothing got him off more than being with someone who stimulated not only his body but his mind. Now that they were away from the prying eyes of others, the extreme intelligence that had shone from the alien's strange eyes hit him hard.

For this guy to have half this stuff meant this wasn't some mindless dolt he was dealing with. He crowded behind the alien and wrapped his arms around the male's taut waist. "I'd rather nibble on something exotic."

He nipped the dark skin at the man's nape. With unexpected force, the Ibbin twisted in his arms until their bodies strained against each other. Savage lust slammed through him. If he thought his cock was hard before, it was nothing to the violent straining he experienced now. The urge to dominate the other male took over.

In an instant, they grappled with one another, trying to exert control. Their grunts, yowls, and roars filled the air, along with the sound of clothing being ripped apart.

Everything in him demanded he subdue the alien to mount him. With a shove, he sent the Ibbin tumbling onto his back on the bed's messy covers. Abiditan jumped on him, eager to make the male submit.

The Ibbin must've expected his move because he brought up a foot that slammed into Abiditan's gut. At the last second, he caught himself to lessen the impact. But the force was hard enough to make him grunt in pain as the Ibbin pushed him off. Good thing he landed on his feet and not his ass.

The Ibbin jumped off the bed. Facing each other, they circled around one another.

Abiditan's erection was livid with anticipation.

When the alien feinted to the right, he fell for it. With his flank exposed, he didn't twist away in time. The Ibbin rammed into him with enough force to smack him onto the rug covering the hard floor. Rolling around in the sparse space, they punched and kicked to gain the upper hand.

None too soon, Abiditan used his body's strength to his advantage and twisted them until he was on top, sitting snugly on the other male's erect groin. Wrapping his arm around his partner's neck, he gave a firm but gentle squeeze.

"I look forward to making you submit to me, Ibbin." Leaning in with his heart pounding with triumph, he whispered into the alien's ear. It will be so delicious when he introduced his cock into the male's warm ass...

He never finished the thought.

The Ibbin pivoted his head to the side, pressing his face against Abiditan's shoulder.

The sting of the male's fangs pierced his skin. "Fuck the galaxy! What was that?" A strange lethargy enveloped him, even as his lust intensified. The sensation took him back to his misspent youth, when he experimented with various hallucinogenic drugs. The crucial difference was all his dominant urges faded as he fell into a pleasurable daze.

Now, the only thing left was the overwhelming drive to please the male under him. Without a thought, he released the Ibbin and sat back on his heels and waited. With a moan, he examined the perfection on the male's noble, handsome face. He'd give anything to kiss those tempting lips, now curved in a predator's anticipation.

"I'm so sorry I had to cheat, *greica*." Qhasheik's tone was anything but conciliatory. "The intoxicant I injected you with is only temporary. Right now, it compels you to obey my demands. But I didn't do it to hurt you. I wanted your guard down so I can love you with the respect and admiration I feel you deserve, but you're not willing to admit."

His deep sigh was quite dramatic. "Not that you and I won't end up fucking. A lot. So much so, it'll be hard for us to walk straight. " He smoothed his palm against Abiditan's heated cheek. "I can't stand the thought no one's ever touched you with anything but shallow lust. I plan to prove to you you're worth that and so much more."

Abiditan moaned when the alien's welcome mouth took over with a tender kiss. Their combined flavors heightened every stroke, every lick of passionate intent he'd never experienced before.

"So, let's take this party to a comfier place." The Ibbin broke the kiss and leaped away. He took Abiditan's hand and pulled him towards the bed.

A small bead of hope thrummed deep in Abiditan's heart.

CHAPTER
SEVEN

Qhasheik gave Abiditan a gentle push to put his soon-to-be lover on his back. With that savory torso tucked under him, he settled onto the juncture of Abiditan's hips. With a wiggle, he rubbed against Abiditan's swollen cock, making the Akurn moan and writhe.

Abiditan lunged upward, but Qhasheik put both palms on him to make him lie back on the bed. "Eh, ya want me, huh?" He chuckled. "Not yet, my eager friend. Not yet. But soon. Let's give the *avvax* time to do its job." He leaned down and kissed and licked the pale side of his mate's neck.

What a shock when the rush of the *avvax* venom filled the oral glands just below his eyes. It was an elixir only produced by the males of his species while in the throes of mating with their soul-pull. The recipient of his venom enjoyed a dose of euphoria and an eagerness to submit to their partner. Since Abiditan was from an alien species, Qhasheik had to make sure his natural stimulant wouldn't harm the male under him.

Abiditan's eyes were clear, but hooded with pleasure. He licked his subtly pink lips with a light-silver tongue. "Are we gonna fuck, or are you just going to talk me to death?"

Qhasheik laughed. Looks like his partner would be just fine. "Hush, *greica*. The only thing you have to do is lay there while I explore this luscious landscape."

With eager hands, Qhasheik got rid of the rest of their clothes.

He thrust his chest out when Abiditan's eyes widened at the sight of his cock as it stood at proud attention. The Akurn sucked in a breath. "By all that's holy in the galaxy, Ibbin. Look at you."

Qhasheik leaned back to allow his stiffened phallus to get the accolades it deserved. With a studious eye on Abiditan's cock, he took a moment to compare. His lover's member was smooth, with a slight bulbous head that glistened in the low light. Tracing a finger along the side of the bobbing dick, he brought the gleaming liquid bubbling from the top to his lips for a taste.

The burst of cool mint with a hint of woolly musk made him moan. He savored the stimulating aroma with his eyes closed. The natural lubricant his partner secreted would double his pleasure when he allowed the male to take the dominant position.

Which wasn't today.

Today was his turn.

He opened his eyes and watched Abiditan study his bobbing erection. An unexpected bout of insecurity swamped him. Comparing his dick to Abiditan's might be stupid, but he couldn't help it. The Akurn's was smooth, but Qhasheik had a slight curve with a tight swirl of cartilage around the staff, which came out when his dick was erect.

The arrow flare of the tip of his penis was round, but embedded inside the top was a hard nub that would extend when he orgasmed. When the nub hit inside of his partner, his seed would make the nub hum in a rounding motion that would hit a female's sensitive spot, or in another male, hit that one area guaranteed to light fireworks.

But first things first. He had an overwhelming desire to taste the male under him. After studying the bounty before him, he leaned to Abiditan's collarbone where it met the shoulder. Pressing his lips there, he suckled and kissed his way to the hollow of his neck.

When Qhasheik visited the other shoulder, the male under him shuddered. Leaving the slightly reddened skin, he made his way back to the well of the Akurn's throat. From there, he started his journey south. When he enclosed his mouth around a gray nipple, he rubbed the softly abrasive surface with his tongue and suckled the eager flesh at the same time.

The Akurn hissed through clenched teeth.

Ah, so sensitive there. "I always wondered why you males had these." He chuckled. "Good to know how susceptible these are. I promise to come back and visit them later."

With a last lick at the tip of his partner's erection, he continued his downward journey, leaving a hot, wet trail along the way. He treated his partner to little darts of pleasure by nipping and pinching the taut landscape, leaving slight pink welts along the way.

Sitting over Abiditan's firm thighs, Qhasheik leaned back with a satisfied leer. He had his partner writhing on the sheets, his cock wobbling as if seeking a source of pleasure. Qhasheik gave a low growl as he watched Abiditan's member produce a pearlescent drop, proving he was doing something right to his alien lover. "Ah, fuck me." He gasped. "That's the most beautiful thing I've ever seen."

"Release me," Abiditan demanded in a hoarse voice. "And I promise it's all yours."

Qhasheik snorted. "Not this time, *greica*. It's important for our first time together that I'm the one embedded deep inside you." He rubbed his hands up and down Abiditan's muscular thighs as he studied the male's stiff prick. He groaned again. "You are one luscious male."

"Holy shit, Ibbin. Stop talking. Why don't you show me instead of talking me to death?"

Seeing the slight pink flush across Abiditan's cheeks and his dilated mismatched eyes, Qhasheik didn't hesitate. He positioned his mouth to enclose the very tip of his partner's dick. He dragged his tongue around the tip before engulfing half the rigid flesh. As he pulled up, he sucked so hard his cheeks hollowed. Releasing his prize, he glanced at the open-mouthed expression on Abiditan's face. "How's that, *greica*?" Not waiting for an answer, he again licked the male's cock from base to end.

It was a pleasure to hear Abiditan's breath explode. Now his partner was ready for the next step. Lifting off the male's legs, Qhasheik settled back on his heels. Reaching between his lover's legs, he gripped the hardened member and slowly rubbed and twisted the self-lubricated cock. "Hold yourself open for me."

Abiditan bent his knees and put his hands on the back of them, spreading his thighs wide. The pinkish glow deepened across his cheeks and spread down his thick neck. "Fuck!"

Qhasheik smiled as the venom made his partner obey without hesitating. "That's it. Now relax and enjoy the ride, my love. I promise to take good care of you," he crooned. "But to do that, I plan on taking my time." He licked the male's dick again as he closed his fist over the base. Instead of giving the release he was sure the other male craved, Qhasheik tightened his grip to dam up the building pressure.

"No! I'm so close." Abiditan squeezed his eyes shut, pushing his hips up as if to rub the inside of Qhasheik's tight hold.

"Not so fast." With a steady hand, he held Abiditan's hips to the bed. He went back to work, stroking the stiffened cock with steady and sure pressure with one hand as his mouth sucked on the top. He massaged hard against the vein pounding on the underside of the straining prick.

All the while, Abiditan alternated between choking sounds that resembled sobs added in a mixture of growling demands.

When Abiditan tensed and his toes curled, Qhasheik pulled his mouth away. Switching hands, he gripped the base of his lover's cock as he used its natural lubricant to smear the juice around Abiditan's puckered entrance. With a croon, he inserted a finger to stretch the tight ring of muscles.

"By the Goddess's balls, unclench for me, *greica*." When Abiditan relaxed, he added another finger to scissor the entrance wider. Probing deeper, he found the rounded lump near the root of the male's penis and stroked. The tortured bellow coming out of the Akurn was music to his ears. Good to know this was familiar territory with an alien partner.

"That's it. Yes, I've waited a long time to see that expression on your face." Qhasheik exulted as he pulled his fingers out. "Yeah, it's time." Still keeping his grip on Abiditan's cock, he swiped around the Akurn's dick to spread the male's liquid over his own cock. Making sure he was ready, he used his other hand to position himself. With slow deliberation, he probed the entrance of the crinkled rosette.

"Relax and let me do the work, you beautiful male. Open for me, and I promise you a reward." When Abiditan's tight hole released, Qhasheik pushed inside, slow and cautious. The sudden jolt of pleasure as he made steady progress inside the tight channel made him breathless. Liquid fire rolled through his balls and amped up his agonizing need. He pulled out and then burrowed deeper, hitting that sweet spot.

Abiditan arched with a howl, and his hands sprang free of their grip on his thighs. Grabbing Qhasheik's ass, he wrapped his legs around the Ibbin's waist. Abiditan's channel squeezed around Qhasheik's dick, which made him grind against the male's prostrate.

"Look at me." Qhasheik demanded when Abiditan's eyes closed. "See who is making love with you." He let go of Abiditan's cock and impaled him as far as he could go inside the other male. Gripping the sides of the Akurn's face, Qhasheik leaned close until their lips were a mere breath apart. He kept his gaze steady on his lover's mismatched eyes to make sure Abiditan didn't miss what he said next.

"Feel the rhythm of our hearts that beat as one." He caressed the pale skin over Abiditan's cheeks with his thumbs. "You and I belong together. Here and now, I pledge myself to you. I am yours for now and always."

Abiditan's eyes widened. "You can't possibly mean that! We barely know each other."

Qhasheik couldn't resist pumping his hips to stroke inside. "There's a legend among my people about old souls finding each other. Recognizing who they are by what's called a soul-pull." He pumped again and snuggled the male underneath him by wrapping his arm around his lover's head to nuzzle his neck. "I never believed that bullshit until I saw you." He nudged Abiditan's head toward him so he could look into those gorgeous, different-colored eyes. "You are my soul-pull."

He closed his eyes and brought their mouths together for a zesty kiss. Slipping his tongue inside, he enticed his lover to taste him back. Stroking his hips in time with the plundering of his tongue, Qhasheik let control go, giving his body free rein to do what felt natural. He drew back and plunged back in. All too soon, his climax beckoned. Just a few more thrusts.

His eyes popped open when Abiditan arched and howled with his eyes squeezed shut. Qhasheik barely registered the tight grip on his ass that squeezed with each thrust. Lucid thought fled as molten elation tightened his balls to flood his cock, splashing inside Abiditan's quivering passage.

Profuse lust poured from his partner's body and splashed against their chests and bellies. Their cries of completion echoed in the small room.

When Qhasheik returned to his senses, pulses of rapture still vibrated through his groin. Having no desire to be separated, he reached down and grabbed the back of his lover's neck to bring him up for a gentle kiss. Their passion eased as the last of their lust faded.

Qhasheik's softened dick slid out as he rested on top of Abiditan, laying his cheek on the Akurn's shoulder to gaze into his lover's mismatched eyes.

No telling how much time passed before the other male spoke. "You don't do things in half measures, do you?"

Qhasheik grinned at him. "Why bother doing anything if it's not worth doing, right?"

Abiditan frowned. "Did you mean anything you said?" He cleared his throat. "I mean, it's okay if it was just part of..."

"Hey, knock it off." He grabbed the sides of Abiditan's head and poured determined sincerity into his voice. "Now you listen to me, you beautiful, beautiful male. You've just admitted I'm not the type of person who doesn't do things half-assed. I meant every word I said about you and me. You can sit there and deny this feeling between us all you want. But never fear, I won't allow it. Even if you push me away, I'll haunt your sweet self for the rest of your days until you learn to accept me. Got it?" He punctuated his statement by giving his partner a bruising kiss.

When he pulled away, his churning stomach calmed at the yearning look that fluttered across Abiditan's pale features. "Good. Now we've settled that, let's get some sleep." He rolled off Abiditan and pulled his back against his chest. "In the morning, I'll do my best to convince you over and over again on how we are meant to be together."

"Well, we'll see how it goes."

Abiditan's rumbling tone made Qhasheik's spent cock twitch.

"But I refuse to agree to anything until you at least tell me your name."

Qhasheik's eyes widened. Holy fuck, he never told this guy his name? Damn, he must be slipping. He chortled and whispered in the male's ear. "My name is Qhasheik. Good to meet ya."

"Likewise." Abiditan gave a regal nod and squeezed Qhasheik's arm around his waist.

A rush of relief made him swallow. For the first time in a long time, Qhasheik found a spark of light in his lonely life. The abuse Abiditan endured throughout his life wouldn't be easy to overcome. Good damn thing he was a wizard at working through unsolvable situations.

Qhasheik closed his eyes. His last thought before drifting off was that it didn't matter what the future brought or the difficulties headed their way. They would face it together. The one thing he was sure of was the solid love he had for the man in his arms.

And thank the All Goddess, life would never be the same again.

CHAPTER EIGHT

The zing of the bloodweep lash being pulled back made Katsuki tense as she waited for the piercing blow. When it hit, the thrash of the three tails with their bulbous tips gave the expected strike of agony. Sucking in a fortifying breath, she bit her bottom lip to stop an anguished scream from escaping.

She'd be damned if she'd give these assholes any satisfaction at hearing how their punishment hurt. Not that she cared how much physical pain these aliens gave her, it never came close to the anguish she suffered every day not knowing where her beloved daughter, Arzea, was.

"That's enough." Her tormentor, Ushpia, clapped his fat hands with a stern demand. "We need to be careful not to damage her too much so even those at the brothel auction won't want to bid for her."

Katsuki slumped between her bound arms that were raised high at her sides by the hovering restraints. Glaring at her tormentor, she made a show of slowly licking the wound she'd made on her mouth.

The metallic taste of her silver blood gave her the courage to look him in the eye when she spat it at his feet.

Ushpia stepped back with a scowl of distaste. His prominent overbite twisted into something comical.

But Katsuki wasn't in the mood to laugh.

"Wrap her up and let's head to the market. I'll be damned if I waste any more time on this *meskim xul*."

Ushipa's lackeys clicked the control on her shackles, freeing her wrists from their binding.

She stumbled, catching herself before she fell face-first on the unyielding tile floor. The stripes of the open wounds on her back stretched and pinched when she straightened. She grunted at the expected pain and crossed her arms over her naked breasts, sharpening the pain further.

"Put this on." Ushpia's minion, Ghunqex, tossed a bland, dirty tunic that had once been blue at her.

Katsuki caught it before it landed over her head. Without a word, she put it on. She wrinkled her nose at the smell of old sweat and urine that rose from the threadbare clothing splotched with age. Well, at least the tunic reached her knees since they hadn't given her any pants or underclothing. She wiggled her dirty feet on the cold ground. She couldn't remember the last time her feet weren't freezing.

"You know, you could've avoided all of this," Ghunquex whispered. "All you had to do was what you were told. Why do you fight me all the time?"

The elderly Akurn might think he was helping her, but he was just as bad as the rest of them. No matter how many times she pleaded and begged for them to help her find her daughter, none of them were smart enough to figure out if they'd did that, she'd be much easier to get along with. She snorted at that ridiculous idea. Okay, even if they did somehow get Arzea, she'd double her efforts to escape. Being a slave on this absurd planet was more than a nightmare. Her days of being the head of the proud House of Enochres might be a distant memory, but they couldn't take away who she was deep inside. She'd run her own successful mining company on a freaking moon, for fuck's sake! She straightened. Assholes hadn't seen what the word persistence meant yet.

Ghunquex didn't expect an answer.

Good thing, 'cause he wasn't getting one. When he came close with a *rappu* gag in his hand, she took in a deep breath before he slapped the damn thing over her mouth. Now, speech was impossible. Not that she'd ever discussed anything with the elderly airhead. She didn't before, and she'd be damned if she did so now.

When Ushpia's other henchman poked her in the back with the blunt end of his laser spear, it forced her to follow her tormentor.

Trudging ahead, Ushpia led their happy little group through the Transkip mirror to the open marketplace in the capital city of Akurn, Eengurra.

No matter how many times she ended up there, it rankled the shit out of her. The only good thing about plodding through the filthy streets on the seedy side of the city was it gave her an opportunity to look for Arzea. Maybe this time she'd get lucky and spot the bright-yellow skin tone of her daughter among the bland paleness of the aliens. Doubtful she'd be able to do anything if she spotted her. But at least she'd know if Arzea was alive or not.

The clientele buying and selling slaves had changed since the last time she was there. The place had its usual crowd of alabaster Akurns, but the splash of different species among them had become few and far between. Probably had something to do with Akurn getting caught in the solar system on the outskirts of the galaxy. It sure limited their chances of conquering other civilizations to get a fresh batch of slaves.

Katsuki looked around. The buying customers seemed to be a desperate, sleazy lot. As Ushpia's little group turned a corner, her eyes widened when she saw where they were headed. No... oh no! She couldn't breathe.

"Good sir." An Akurn female stepped in front of Ushpia, blocking them from moving. The woman wore the finest materials with only her bluebell eyes peeking above the veil hiding the lower part of her face.

Katsuki sucked a long breath through her nose. Her mouth would've dropped open if it hadn't been sealed with the *rappu* gag. Seeing a female Akurn out in public was a rarity, even with that contingent of male slaves following behind her. This woman was just asking to get herself killed as an example to warn other females against walking around in public.

"May I inquire what you plan on doing with this exotic female?" She waved an elegant hand in Katsuki's direction.

Ushpia was a pig, but he wasn't stupid. After giving the female an up-and-down perusal, he checked out the group of males surrounding her. He paused and studied one of the bulky guards, who wore a full head helmet with his body covered in armor. After a tense moment, he must've decided it was in his best interest to play along. He turned his attention back to the female.

"This here, ah, *female*—" He coughed when he stressed the last word. "—is worthless. She's slated to be sold in the pleasure-houses auction. Why? What's it to you?" He folded his arms and leaned back. Any time now, he'd tap his foot. Patience wasn't one of his virtues.

"Is that so?" The female studied Katsuki with a quick glance. "I can understand why you say that. She looks like she'd be more trouble than she's worth."

Ushpia snorted as he rubbed the rectangle beard on his chin. "I wouldn't say that." He gave Katsuki a warning glance. "It's just that her usefulness for me has ended. Why? Are you interested?"

The woman nodded. "My father, one of the largest landowners on the southern continent, requested I search for any exotic, alien females I can find for him." Her eyelids lowered, letting her thick lashes hide her expression. "And since I am an ever-dutiful daughter, I do as my father commands."

"As you should." Ushpia grunted. "So, what do you have in mind?" His eyes narrowed with a greedy gleam.

The female gave a dramatic sigh. "I'm afraid I've depleted the allotted funds my father gave me, and I haven't gotten as many slaves as he demanded." Wiping a single tear from the corner of her eye, she leaned closer to him and whispered as she placed a palm on the male's exposed forearm. "I don't suppose you'd consider a trade?"

Ushpia stiffened before his whole demeanor changed.

Katsuki had seen nothing like it.

Gone was the bully who walked around like he had a huge stick up his ass, and in its place was some guy who had turned into mellow pile of goo. The steel blue-green glint in his eyes softened, and his stern frown turned into a winsome smile.

"Now, that's a good boy." The woman patted his arm as she whispered to him. "Let's go over there and talk in private. Shall we?"

"Edinni." This warning came from the gargantuan man Ushpia had studied earlier.

"Hush, Damuzi." She admonished the male with a dismissive wave of her hand. "I promise we'll leave after this one." She nodded to

Katsuki. "Why don't you stay and guard her while this gentleman and I have a quick conversation?" She said this loud enough so that Ushpia's guards would follow her and their master.

Katsuki couldn't believe it when Ushpia strolled away with the Akurn as if he had nothing else to do.

He followed Edinni with his head bowed, listening to whatever the woman said.

A massive male stepped in front of her and blocked her sight of whatever the woman and Ushpia were doing.

She tilted her head back to gape at the giant who stood with a glower and his immense arms crossed.

Because of his helmet, his booming voice had a tinny echo. "Listen, female. There isn't much time, so pay attention. My companion and I are leaving Akurn to start our own city away from these assholes on Earth's moon. We need able-bodied people to join us to help build it. It'll be hard work, and there won't be any luxuries. We'll be lucky if we survive at all. But at least I'm offering you a chance of freedom." He tilted his head toward the brothel compound Ushpia intended to take her to. "Unless you'd rather end up there."

She would've smiled at his snort of derision if her lips weren't bound.

"You go there, and I guarantee you'll be dead in less than six months." He took a step back and put his fists on his hips. "So, what's it to be? You want to come with us for a chance to live a free life, or would you rather go with him and die?"

Well, wasn't he just the most eloquent conversationalist? Katsuki glanced around his wide frame at the sordid compound that housed the disreputable pleasure houses. She'd vowed she'd rather kill herself than endure life there. But if she left Akurn to live on Earth's moon, how would she find her daughter? Regarding the male hidden behind his elaborate battlesuit, she suspected he hid his true nature so he wouldn't stand out among the pale Akurns. She wasn't stupid enough to believe she'd gain complete freedom with them, but at least it'd give her a chance to regain her health after the endless years of slavery had taken it from her. And with careful planning, it'd give her a chance to come back and look for her daughter.

"Well?" He nodded to where the female, Edinni, looked like she was wrapping up her conversation with Ushpia. "Give me a nod, and we'll leave before Edinni's drug wears off on that disgusting *idimmu*."

As if by magic, the pain and weight in her chest lightened. For the first time in a long time, she was getting a break. Okay, here was her chance. She'd grab it before it they changed their minds. Giving the male a pointed stare, she nodded.

CHAPTER NINE

A biditan almost choked on the giddy excitement twisting his guts. Another hour, and he and Qhasheik would have two whole days to themselves. Two glorious days of alone time with his love. It took some doing, but he made sure the co-rulers of Azadi could do without either of them then. After haggling and negotiating with their respective overseers on the project, they'd finally secured the break both desperately needed.

This last year had been especially grueling. If they didn't take the time to reconnect, their relationship might suffer. Life with the Ibbin was too good to let that happen.

Humming an old song, he double-checked the latest schematics on his computer.

An unexpected feminine voice spoke behind him.

"Are you Abiditan?"

A chill raced down his spine. He exhaled and turned around. His eyes widened at the exotic sight framed in the arched doorway. There stood one of the most beautiful females he'd ever seen. Bright-yellow skin was offset by the creamy brown curtain of straight hair. Strands of gold and auburn highlights framed a face only a goddess could produce. Her nose was a delicate line that ran smooth from her eyes to the tip, where it turned up with a gentle curve. Her jawline was a powerful frame for her high cheekbones.

But it was her eyes that held him speechless. Instead of a pupil, hers featured a solid sea of stunning teal he swore shone with an inner light. Thick, luscious, chocolate-colored lashes framed those eyes and matched her arched eyebrows. She held him in a sensual thrall until she blinked.

"Hey, if you're not Abiditan, do you know where I can find him?" She crossed her arms over bountiful breasts and tilted her head.

He swallowed hard. "Yes." Coherent thought was nowhere near his mouth.

She tapped her foot. "Yes, what? Yes, you're Abiditan, or yes, you know where he is?"

"Um, yes." He cleared his throat. "I mean, yes, I'm Abiditan. Can I help you with something?" Like help you get naked.

She frowned with a dubious expression. "Oookaaay. Look, I hate to bother you, but Damuzi said I should ask you about this contradiction in the layout of the main conference room." She came closer, then stopped. Her nostrils flared and with a gasp she touched her throat. A flush of gold spread across her cheeks and neck as her luminous teal eyes scanned over his body. When her gaze settled back to look at him in the eyes, she licked her bottom lip, making the darker gold skin shiny.

That's all it took. He was a goner. The intense pull this female had on him was right up there with what he experienced with Qhasheik. Different, but no less fierce. With an inborn instinct, he yearned to take her to meet his lover. With sudden insight, he knew this female was an important part missing in his life. Someone he never knew he needed. And if he felt this way, no doubt Qhasheik would too. They were so in sync with each other, they rarely disagreed about anything.

He lessened the distance between himself and the alluring female. Her subtle feminine scent combined with her tantalizing body warmth enveloped him in a blanket of homecoming. Inhaling, he basked in the unfamiliar floral bouquet mixed with the heady aroma of musky female.

He grabbed her hands in his and took the chance to give her knuckles a kiss. "What is your name, lovely female?" Wow, that was all kinds of cheesy. Thank all that was holy in the galaxy Qhasheik didn't hear him speak like a lovelorn loser.

Good thing she seemed to like it. Her stern demeanor softened, and she brought her body close enough to touch his. "I'm Katsuki, handsome."

Oh, hell's balls. His knees weakened when she called him handsome. "Katsuki." Abiditan rolled the fascinating word around his tongue. "Are you free this evening? I would love to take you to my place where we can get to know one another better." He turned her wrist over and placed a kiss on the soft skin. "I'll even treat you to last meal."

Katsuki's teasing smile caused something to twist low inside him.

"I don't believe it. An Akurn male who can cook? Oh my, the universe is going to implode anytime."

By the dung of a *goraxag*! Could this female be more perfect for him and Qhasheik?

Where was that male?

Qhasheik fumed as he sat at their small kitchen table and tapped a finger on the hard surface. Twin candles placed in the middle framed an expensive bottle of *luskanii* between them.

I swear if he let someone talk him into doing something, I'm going to...

The sound of laughter caught his attention. Was that a... female voice? The dulcet tones of her giggling made his cock twitch and his heart thrum. *Hmm*, what delightful treat had his mate brought home? He faced the doorway, swiping his sweaty palms down the side of his tunic. He, who made it a point to never be nervous about anything, was sweating as if his life was about to change.

Holding his breath, he watched the door dissolve open. Aaand... there she was. The last piece of the soul-pull. Qhasheik never mentioned the hole he sensed in his union with Abiditan. At all costs, he avoided feeding into his mate's insecurities. Looked like that was the wrong call. He should've trusted Abiditan and the strength of their union. His face heated in shame.

"And this is..."

Abiditan didn't get another word in before Katsuki gasped and rushed to Qhasheik and leaped on him.

He grabbed her just in time as she wrapped her muscular legs around his waist and grabbed his horns. Oh, fuck. Now the heat rushing over his face and down his neck came from a different emotion. He yanked her close and planted a fervent kiss on her seductive mouth.

She opened and plunged her tongue inside to dance with his.

They both moaned in unison. Hot bolts of lust fought off any intelligent thought.

"You..." She jerked away and peppered his cheeks with a kiss. "You..." A kiss to his forehead. She turned and glared at Abiditan. "What took you guys so long to find me?" She turned back to

Qhasheik and narrowed her pupilless eyes. "Since you are both my *aruu*, it was your duty to find me!" Her admonishment came out in a wobbly voice as clear, silver tears gathered and rolled down her cheeks.

Qhasheik's translator announced the word *aruu* meant "eternal soul mate".

"Forgive us, *myressci*." He crooned the endearment into her ear.

Calling her his heart's treasure made her sniffle.

When Abiditan joined the hug at Katsuki's back, Qhasheik wrapped an arm around the male's waist as the female reached behind her to plant a hand at his neck. "You're right." He said. "Please forgive us, we are nothing but humble males who should've scoured the galaxy for you." He squeezed her firm buttocks and rubbed her fiery core over his fierce erection. "But now that we are together, our soul-pull is complete."

"No." She unwrapped her legs to stand and gave him a gentle shove. She clutched Abiditan's arm around her waist. "The *aruu* won't be complete until we join." With a mulish frown, she stepped out of Abiditan's hold.

Crossing her arms, she grabbed the end of her tunic and lifted it over her head. Dark-gold nipples tipped her firm, ample breasts. The gentle glow of her yellow skin covered her tantalizing torso that was firm and compact, with a curving waist that flared to tempting hips begging any male to hold on to them as he pounded into her sex. With a bold stare, she kicked off her low-heeled slippers and shimmied out of her loose pants before kicking them away.

His eyes zeroed in on the fine down of chestnut curls at the apex of her glistening nether lips.

"By all that's holy in the galaxy." Abiditan growled. He prowled behind the naked female and put his hands at the sides of her neck, massaging the back of her head to lift the silky curtain of hair. "Have you ever seen anything so magnificent in your life, Qhasheik?" Leaning down, he kissed the skin between her neck and shoulder.

She moaned, arched back, and wrapped a hand around the back of his head.

Qhasheik's mouth watered. Her skin had to be as soft and fragrant as it looked. He couldn't wait to be a part of that embrace. Shortening the distance, he put his hands over Abiditan's and captured her mouth in a heated kiss. Pulling back, he murmured against her moist skin. "My loves, shall we take this somewhere more horizontal?"

"Only if you're naked first."

Her demand told him everything he needed to know. This was not some shy flower waiting to be told what to do. She was as dominant as he and Abiditan were. He shivered at the possibilities.

Katsuki closed her eyes and took in a cleansing breath. When her racing nerves steadied, she opened her eyes again. Observing the two males bracketing her, a sense of peace took over. Here was the haven she'd never dared to hope for in this never-ending nightmare she'd endured for so long. Even if she found herself back in Narkata, she wouldn't have the sense of completeness she found with them.

The minute she set eyes on the deep-purple alien, something deep inside clicked. By the shocked expression on his inky face, he knew it too. She had zero doubt the *aruu* wouldn't have taken hold if all three of them weren't together.

The only thing missing would be the mating circlet of her people, the *Qabuth-Kun*, a silver crown a Runihura male rips from his head to place on his *aruu*. Now it became quite clear why she never desired that outward symbol to show who she belonged with. In fact, she'd always thought it was a barbaric custom. A genetic leftover from her people's past when females suffered under an extreme patriarchy society.

To make this binding complete, she had to absorb their seed into her. Then the final bond would unite them as eternal mates. Once that was done, nothing could ever separate them.

"Well?" She put a little extra sway into her hips as she headed toward the massive bed at the end of the room with its jumbled covers and plump pillows strewn about. Putting her hands under her hair at the back of her head, she lifted and rumpled the heavy strands to flow down her back. She looked over her shoulder at the two males standing there with identical expressions of lust and awe. She chuckled. "Come on, boys. I promise this won't hurt one bit." As soon as her back leg touched the bed, she gracefully lowered herself and turned sideways. Keeping her thighs together, she crossed one ankle over the other. Pulling her long hair over her shoulder caused the strands to whisper over her erect nipples. For an added invitation, she licked her lips and stared at the impressive tents they sported in their pants.

As if a switch was thrown, both jumped into action. In their haste to join her, most of their clothing didn't survive the ripping and tearing as they strove to get as naked as she was. When they traversed the short distance to the bed, they were both nude as the day they were born. Their muscled chests rose and fell with deep breaths.

She put a finger to her lips to study her new companions. They were fine, fine, fine. No... more than fine. They were both perfect. Damn, she doubted she'd last long once their hard bodies touched her. That's all she'd need to explode in ecstasy. She sucked in a breath and tightened her legs as if that would give her strength.

"Beautiful lady, lie back and let us get to know you." Abiditan's voice was low as the bed dipped when he crawled behind her.

She fell into his arms.

He gently lowered her back to the soft surface with her head nestled on his lap.

Qhasheik took advantage and spread her legs and he sat on his heels between them. He ran his dark-skinned, sizable hands up her thighs and created a trail of chill bumps over her legs, belly, and breasts.

Not to be outdone, Abiditan stroked her shoulders and leaned down to kiss one. His lustrous, platinum hair caressed and tickled her skin as he moved.

A spicy animal scent permeated the air, a strange mixture of the two of them. Abiditan carried a lighter spicy flavor while Qhasheik had a zesty base note of male musk.

Abiditan captured one swollen nipple between his teeth and flicked the tip with his tongue while his fingers worked her other peak. He sucked her areola around the puckered skin with amazing agility.

Meanwhile, Qhasheik stroked her pussy with a forefinger, spreading her wetness over her extended clit.

The gentle torture he created made her whimper, which got louder with every stroke. Closing her eyes, Katsuki plunged into a world of pleasure. Abiditan's mouth and hands tormented her breasts, alternating between tiny twinges of pain and heated rapture, while Qhasheik's fingers scissored in and out of her pussy.

His strokes were rough one moment and then gentle the next. The burgeoning climax tightened when his scraping tongue flicked over her clit, then alternated with giving her a gentle nip. When his lips surrounded it to suck hard, she was just shy of exploding under the dual pressure her lovers created.

Cool air hit.

They'd pulled away.

She growled. Who said they could take their warm bodies away? Her eyes flew open. Harsh, nasty noises rumbled out of her throat as her body thrummed with painful yearning. The urge for release tightened everything low inside. Glaring at them both kneeling beside her on the bed, she tried to sit up. She couldn't move.

"What the hell?" She yanked her arms, but they didn't budge. And damn, her legs wouldn't work either. She tilted her head to look down her body and found a thin silver chain was strapped to each ankle and wrist. Delicate-looking manacles that were stronger than any shackle she'd ever experienced before coming to Akurn. Since the damn things were remote controlled, she didn't have a prayer of getting out of them until her captors released them.

Katsuki opened her mouth to demand they let her go, but Qhasheik captured her lips in a blistering kiss. Their combined tastes coated his probing tongue, causing her desire to override everything else.

Then it was Abiditan's turn. He pressed her thighs wide.

The feel of his mouth on her sex relaxed her enough for her desire to roar back with a vengeance. When his slick tongue lapped inside her pussy, she pushed her hips up to rub her engorged clit against him.

All. Most. There. A throb of emptiness low inside pinched hard and tight.

With one last suckle, Abiditan leaned back and gave her sensitive sex a sharp slap.

A roaring thunderclap of rapture detonated. A climactic hurricane held Katsuki and caused her insides to spasm. Tossing her head back and forth, she moaned and strained against her restraints.

Abiditan pressed the tip of his cock into her. He slipped in with ease because of her natural lubrication mixed with his.

As he filled her swollen channel, her sensual ache rolled back with a vengeance. The feel of his overwhelming penetration brought Katsuki back to an orgasmic, trembling edge. His first thrust was hard and wonderful.

"Open for me, my *myressei*."

The rumble of Qhasheik's command didn't register. When he rubbed the tip of his cock against her parted lips, she latched on, and her breath caught. With him on all fours, his erect phallus was poised right where she wanted it. Her mouth watered as she connected with the tantalizing prize. She sucked the tip before yanking her head away. "Release me."

There was no shame in her guttural tone. The urge to explore the tantalizing single nub below his penis went along with wanting to touch as much of him as she could. She didn't know or care which one of them did as she requested, but when her limbs became heavy as the suspension hold disappeared, she wrapped her legs around Abiditan's plunging hips while caressing Qhasheik's ass to pull him closer.

They both moaned, and their sensual movements faltered for a heartbeat.

Not waiting, she closed her lips over the jutting flesh that took up her line of sight, taking as much as she could. She rolled her tongue over the rigid length before letting most of it slip out then sucking it back in. The circular ridges looped around his cock pulsated with each swipe of her tongue. His deep groan was music to her ears.

Abiditan ramped up his efforts, driving deeper and deeper to solidify his claim.

Not to be outdone, Qhasheik probed his cock into her willing mouth with care. His flexing buttocks undulated under her kneading hands. Katsuki mewled at the bombarding sensations ramping through her and taking over. Abiditan bore down on the nerve cluster in her quivering pussy until she forgot what she was doing. Instinct alone guided her as her coming climax sharpened. She shuddered and in mindless desperation sucked on Qhasheik's pulsating cock.

"Now, damnit, Abiditan!" Qhasheik pulled his straining cock free from her mouth.

She wailed with her treat taken away.

Abiditan's thrusts became erratic until one last hard shove had him shouting.

The force of his release propelled her into another burning inferno. The hard splash of his seed hit something hidden inside her, causing unexpected explosions to reach the end of her toes and cramping fingers. She half expected her hair to be on fire. Throughout her body, tiny explosions expanded before dissipating.

When Abiditan moved off her, she moaned at the loss before Qhasheik's fevered body took his place.

He stared down at her with a dark, dangerous expression.

She shivered as his unusual eyes narrowed until the red irises disappeared into the sea of blackness.

His lips pulled back, revealing his double-rowed eyeteeth fangs.

The intensity of his gaze held her captive. If she'd been in her right mind, she might've been terrified of the apex predator ready to mount her. Good thing she wasn't in her right mind. She grasped the loop of his curling horns and pulled him down for a fierce kiss. In response, he shoved his massive cock into her willing pussy. The feel of his wide flesh piercing her made her throw her head back, breaking the kiss with a resounding shriek of pleasure. Her body now hummed with remembered ecstasy and demanded more.

As Qhasheik's hips jackhammered into her, she clutched her legs around him. Pressing her heels into his ass, she urged him to go faster and harder.

"As my lady demands." The incoherent words came out garbled, hard to understand. He pulled out and flipped her over. His brawny arm wrapped around her waist as he put her on her hands and knees. With her ass in the air, he slid back in, his movements exact and powerful.

The new position gave his cock the perfect place to piston against the extra-sensitive nerve cluster in her channel. Sexual excitement ballooned once again. When he circled her clit with his fingertips, she stiffened and strained to get even closer. As he drove into her with steady, mighty strokes, she pumped back. Katsuki's elation climbed higher, crested, fell, and then soared when he pinched her straining nub. She detonated with a staggering force unlike anything she'd ever experienced before.

Qhasheik gave one last shove before he shouted at the ceiling.

The feel of his body rippling in his climax made tiny tremors pulse through her. His cock jerked and throbbed inside her as a substantial pouring of his cum thrummed into her.

He slammed once more into her with a yell.

When coherent thought floated back, she smiled. After getting stranded and being made a slave on Akurn, she'd finally found where and to whom she truly belonged. Goddess help anyone who ever came between her and her *aruus*.

"*Nurens bhot'is erqen don lyari, Aruu.*" She spoke in her native tongue to solidify their three-way union. "My eternal soul is now intertwined with yours. We are one."

There. Now they were eternal soul mates until the day they died.

CHAPTER TEN

*P*resent Day - Aboard the spaceship Nergal, heading to the planet
Runihura with the disgraced tyrant Sub Prince Murduk in stasis.

Qhasheik couldn't help it. He crossed his arms and scowled at his
female. "I thought you said you came from a place called Narkata." He
gestured to the floating monitor showcasing a prominent, well-known
member of the Federation Consortium in exquisite detail.

The myriad colors of red, blue, green, and brown snuggled in a swirl
of clouds streaming over the surface.

"I've never been there myself, but everyone in the sane galaxy knows
what Runihura looks like. And any male with half intelligence knows
to stay as far away from there as he can."

"Runihura?" Abiditan rubbed the bridge of his nose. "I don't think
I've ever heard of it."

Qhasheik snorted. "Of course not. Your back-ass, narrow-minded
planet might be the exact opposite, but they were at least smart enough
to not go near that death trap."

"Hey!" Katsuki jumped out of the chair at the communications
station with her hands on her hips. "There's nothing wrong with my
planet. At least we never went around making war on everybody."

She rubbed the back of her neck. "But I should warn you about something."

When she bit her bottom lip, Qhasheik braced himself.

"Runihura doesn't tolerate aliens, especially unclaimed males, to stay there for any length of time." She dropped her arms and gave him a stern look. "So while we're there, you'll have to behave yourself. Good thing I'm the head of the House of Enochres and have the absolute say on who lives on the Narkata moon." She walked around the circular navigational console and stopped in front of him.

Even without pupils in her neon-turquoise eyes, Qhasheik had no trouble feeling her steely gaze on him.

"You know as well as I do, if I'd told those assholes on Akurn where I was from, they'd have targeted Runihura and stripped it of all its resources. Then they'd destroy it just like they did Peinuewei." She wrapped her arms around Qhasheik's waist and laid her forehead against his chest. They'd been together so long, she always knew that whenever someone spoke about his planet, he spiraled into grief.

He closed his eyes at the memory of the Akurns destroying it. Taking a deep breath, he let the tension go. Stroking the back of her head, he allowed the silky strands to calm him as he breathed in her subtle, feminine fragrance.

"When we were first seized, I distracted them with coordinates to an old base we'd abandoned centuries before, and called it Narkata. It was the first name I could come up with, even though that's the name of the moon my family owns. That way, I made sure those assholes left my planet alone."

Her voice rumbled against his skin, causing it to pebble. Damn it! Just the whisper of her soft breath against his skin made him randy as an untried youth. He squeezed the tight globes of her ass and rubbed her groin against his. In bliss, he rested his chin on the top of her head.

"Thank the Goddess I found out Arzea did the same thing when she thought I was dead."

It was a shock to see the pragmatic Katsuki so giddy with joy when she talked to her daughter during their voyage to Runihura.

She told him she didn't want to leave Akurn after finding her daughter after all this time, but she'd admitted to him and Abiditan it was for the best. It gave Arzea a chance to begin her new life at Amil's side, helping him rule a planet. Being pregnant with his heir made it even more bittersweet. At least the two of them spoke every day to get to know each other all over again.

Katsuki hugged him tighter. "It wasn't too long after that their rogue days ended when their greed got them caught in Earth's solar system."

Oh yeah, she was still talking about Akurn as she rubbed his lower back and rested her cheek against his chest. She turned her head to look at Abiditan with a small smile. "No offense, my *suharus*."

Abiditan shrugged. "You don't have to apologize for the truth, khoshgel." He leaned back in his chair and crossed an ankle over a knee. "Well, since Qhasheik and I are obviously not from Runihura, are we going to Narkata instead?"

Katsuki pulled out of Qhasheik's arms with a soft, seductive smile. She grasped the end of one of his horns and rubbed her thumb over the tip.

A shot of lust tightened low, making his dick jerk to attention. Yep, all it took was one touch from her, and anything that resembled smarts went bye-bye.

"No, we're going to take Murduk to the council, like we promised Queen Inanna. We'll let them decide what to do with him. Besides, I don't want that cold bastard anywhere near my ancestral home."

"I don't get it. Why we don't jettison the fucker out the airlock and be done with it?" Qhasheik growled. It wasn't the first time he'd suggested it. Why they put themselves through all this horseshit was ridiculous. Besides, once they landed on Runihura, he had a sneaking suspicion their precious alone time might become a thing of the past. The rumors he'd heard about this place made him more than nervous. "That way we can go to the bedchamber and finish what you started here." He licked her parted lips. She sucked in a breath as her eyelids went half-mast.

"Attention alien craft. You have illegally entered Runihura space. You have one click to state your intentions before we unleash the full force of our armament upon you." The stern female voice was without inflection.

Shit! Cock-blocked. "Damn, that shrill voice would yank any guy out of the mood." Qhasheik hated it when he was right about something so wrong. "Love the greeting. "Talk to me now or we'll kill you"." He mimicked in a high-falsetto tone.

"Oh, hush, Qhasheik." Katsuki admonished with a gentle shove and headed back to her communication station.

Well, hell. Some days he swore his name was *OhHushQhasheik*. There went playtime.

Katsuki opened a channel to respond. "Attention Runihura Base five. This is High Aspect Katsuki Bargouda requesting permission to land."

A tense silence before the disembodied voice answered. "Inconceivable. We demand verification by vid to accompany voice recognition."

Katsuki glanced over her shoulder and gave him and Abiditan a wide smile. She preened and fluffed her long hair at the back of her head. The curtain of silk flowed smoothly down her back. "Think I look okay?"

Qhasheik snorted. Katsuki was the least-vain female he'd ever met. Appearances were never high on her agenda. "You'll do." He crossed his arms and played along.

"Damn, Q. You're such an idiot. Only you would pass up an opportunity to tell her how gorgeous she is." Abiditan sat back in his chair and clasped his hands behind his head. He dropped his leg to the floor and crossed his ankles. "Katsuki, my Eternal Mate, you are ever the most beautiful female in nine galaxies."

Qhasheik shook his head. "You're such a suck-up."

Katsuki giggled. The female never giggled.

He frowned. Now he was in deep shit.

"Thank you, ulvot. For that, when we get together again, we'll snap the Lover's Snare on him." She thumbed in his direction. "Maybe prolonging his release will teach him the proper way to address a lady."

Qhasheik's dick jerked in complete agreement. Hope was on the horizon after all. One of his favorite things was being dominated by his lovers. Occasionally, of course. He crossed his arms and narrowed his gaze, giving them plenty of fang when he smiled. "We will see if you can make it happen." Fuck, he couldn't wait.

Giving him a sultry smile, she flicked her hair over her shoulder and faced her communication console. "Opening vid now." She waved the two-way screen open.

The headshot of an elderly female caught him by surprise. Never in a million years would he've imagined a species whiter than an Akurn. This otherworldly woman's skin was so porcelain white it had no pigmentation. Her deep-purple eyes contained no pupil and matched the bluish-purple of her hair. Almost the same color as his skin tone.

The woman looked at Katsuki as her eyes widened. "High Aspect? Is that really you?"

Katsuki's grin was genuine. "It's wonderful to see you again, Vioy-cleia. How is your family?"

"They're all fine." She rubbed her eyes as if she couldn't believe what she was seeing. "But, how...?"

"Status, Chief Tech!" Another female came into the line of sight. This one had brick-red skin offset by hair as dark as midnight. Her neon, pupilless, black eyes had an eerie glow.

Vioycleia stiffened as she pointed to Katsuki. "Honored one, it's High Aspect Katsuki Bargouda, back from the dead!"

Katsuki couldn't have been more shocked if she woke up in the arms of the Lady of All Life herself. Here she stood in front of the ruling senate of Runihura that was declaring her dead. Legally speaking.

Funny how being gone so long created annoying consequences. Looked like her greedy bitch of a cousin, Eiael, didn't even bother to wait the normal grief period of a year before declaring her dead. That done, she confiscated the assets of the House of Enochres after three months. Three months!

She clenched her hands into fists under her crossed arms and glared at the Magistrates of Runihura. Somebody on this ruling panel had to be in on it. No way could incompetent, lazy Eiael take over Katsuki's rich territory on her own. No matter how often the damn backbiter insinuated Narkata should've been hers.

"Honorable Magistrates." She bit the side of her cheek to suppress her impatience as she addressed the four women looking down on her and her men with regal disdain. Look at them. Arrogant politicians trying to assert their power by sitting on a raised platform. "As you can plainly see, I'm not dead. And I assure you, neither is my daughter, Arzea."

She refused to look behind her at Qhasheik's snort. So far, he'd been the poster boy for subservient males. No telling how long that'd last.

"I'm glad to hear that about your daughter. Is she with you?"

This came from Magistrate Islebell, a distant cousin from the house of Enochres. The elderly matron had sat on the judicial ruling body for hundreds of years. Gray streaked through her caramel-brown hair, and her face had long lost its youthful glow. But her turquoise gaze remained bright and clear. "No matter." She waved a palm up when Katsuki opened her mouth. "I'm afraid our hands are tied. The law states that after a formal declaration of death, the person no longer exists. Therefore, neither you nor your daughter have any claims as citizens of Runihura."

The other two magistrates nodded in agreement while Magistrate Horisa yawned with her eyes half closed.

Damn, she sure hoped she wasn't boring the female.

A commotion at the back of the room made everyone turn around.

Katsuki did a double take. Who in the world was that corpulent slug waddling toward them? Could that be...? No, it couldn't. Holy crap, it was! Well, didn't this make things so much better?

The repugnant cow heading toward them was her cousin, Eiael. Freakin' woman had to have gained two hundred pounds since the last time Katsuki'd seen her. And the added weight was not her friend. Her once-proud beauty was engulfed by excess flesh. Her beady, burnt-orange eyes were hard to see because they were buried by her inflated cheeks. Her pug nose poked out from the folds of flesh on either side.

Out of the corner of her eye, Katsuki noticed Abiditan and Qhasheik stepping closer to her. She must've given them some unconscious notion she needed their help. Either to calm her down or lend a hand when she attacked Eiael. Not that they could've done much with their feet and hands shackled.

"She has no claim to Narkata! I demand you throw her and her disgusting males off the planet." Eiael stomped in front of the raised dais and addressed the magistrates. "There's no reason to have this impostor running around making outrageous allegations."

Katsuki ignored the heat flooding her face and neck. "Outrageous allegations? What, that I'm alive?" She held her temper back by a mere thread. "I'm obviously not dead, you stupid piece of *diofokyo*."

Eiael didn't even look her way. "My legal claim to Narkata is without question. It is binding and unbreakable." She waved at the small group of males following her. "Where is my seat?" She snapped her fingers in quick succession. "I shouldn't have to ask for it."

One of her slaves, a male with the coloring of the House of Aryennis, rushed to provide his mistress with a massive chair that had sat flush against the nearest wall. Good thing the snowy white male had enough muscles to fulfill Eiael's demand.

She flopped onto the cushy seat without looking behind her. "Don't make me ask for what I need again."

Clueless idiot didn't notice the male's cheeks had turned a thin shade of gray along with his pinched lips.

He clenched his hands into fists and backed away to join the other males she'd brought with her.

"Damn, the guys here sure are huge." Qhasheik murmured under his breath.

Katsuki suppressed a smile. She'd forgotten most of the Runihura males averaged eight feet tall. Good. Maybe him noticing that would stop her love from doing or saying something stupid. She doubted it, but one could hope.

Eiael shifted in her chair, as if trying to find a cozy spot.

Time to take this to a higher level before the bitch got comfortable.

Katsuki crossed her arms and stood in front of her annoying relative. "I demand to see Queen Arelle or Princess Inocenci to settle this absurd claim."

Horsia's eyes popped open. Her neon-brown gaze focused on Katsuki. "I'm afraid my sister-by-marriage is indisposed. The grief of Princess Inocenci's kidnapping has become too much for her." She sat straight in her throne-like chair and gripped the ornate armrests until her midnight skin darkened. "No one is allowed to disrupt her. I am the acting Queen until further notice."

Out of the corner of her eye, Katsuki noticed Magistrate Fehlel sit back with a satisfied smirk. Ah, that had to be who helped Eiael wrestle enough power to take over Narkata. Now those rumors about the chalky-white female working to undermine the ruling house of Runihura made sense. Looked like things are well on their way for that to happen. "And what is being done to locate the missing Princess?"

Eiael slapped her hand on the armrest with a laugh. "Why, they let good old Prince Aylzrunth off planet to look for her!" She laughed harder. "Why they let a male do a female's job is beyond me. But hey, he's been gone long enough that things are finally getting done."

"Shut up, Eiael." Horsia snapped. She turned her attention to Katsuki. "Since I am Acting-Queen, I have the ultimate word here. I deny your claim."

"I second that denial." Fehlel's smirk turned into an evil leer.

Katsuki watched the remaining two magistrates.

The deep wine red of Magistrate Treva's face tightened with pursed lips as she nodded. Her shining white eyes narrowed at Horsia.

A sign of disapproval if Katsuki wasn't mistaken. Taking a deep breath, she faced Magistrate Islebell. She slumped when the woman gave a curt nod of agreement with a heavy sigh.

Well, fuck. That left only one option for her. "I declare the Challenge of Yavanna to Eiael for all rights and privileges in the House of Enochres. My claim is just by our ancient laws scribed from the Lady of All Life at the dawn of our illustrious civilization. Even though you've declared me dead and a non-citizen, I invoke the rite under her name. And as a female under her protection, you cannot deny me."

The silence in the chamber was heavy until Eiael jumped up and screeched. "No! No way is that repulsive *hysta* allowed to claim Yavanna!" She pointed a finger at Katsuki. "I won't have it!" She stomped her foot and put her meaty fists on her wide hips.

Islebell's slow smile told Katsuki she was on the right track. She threw her shoulders back and faced Horsia.

At first, the woman frowned as she tapped a finger on the armrest. After a quick glance at Fehlel, she shrugged. "I see no legal reason to deny your request."

"NO!" Eiael shouted.

"However." Islebell interjected. "Because of the unusual circumstances, we will outline how the challenge will be conducted. First, no champions are allowed. Each of you must personally enter the battle."

"I won't..."

"Second." Treva ignored Eiael and picked up the narrative. "Each candidate is only allowed one weapon. No blasters or any device that kills from a distance. This is a personal, vicious fight that could lead to death. If a kill doesn't happen, first blood has to occur for a clear winner to be declared. Once that is announced, the loser not only forfeits all rights and privileges to the house of Enochres, but will be banished from Runihura and our territories forever."

Magistrate Fehlel leaned forward and clasped her fingers into a tight fist on her lap. "I want to amend this a bit. If you lose"—she glared at Katsuki—"we'll banish you, but keep your males to be auctioned off at the highest bidder." Her puke-green eyes gleamed with fanatical lust.

Fucking bitch. One day, Katsuki was gonna bash that sly sneer off Fehlel's face. Even if it was the last thing she ever did.

CHAPTER ELEVEN

R elieved of his shackles, Abiditan was free to watched Katsuki with his arms crossed and a scowl as she donned her battle gear. At least what there was of it. He'd seen vids of Earth women on the beaches of Rio with more clothes.

This primitive-looking outfit had just enough material to lift and hold her bountiful breasts, and the thong draped over her hips left the globes of her buttocks bare while a panel of black leather draped over her sex. Nestled over her forearms were matching leather shields held together by gold buckles.

She'd wound her glorious cinnamon-colored hair into a tight bun. When she first started putting on the ridiculous outfit, she explained instead of her formfitting battlesuit, she'd rather wear as little as possible to stop Eiael from claiming forfeit because Katsuki had something hidden in her clothing.

"Holy shit, Katsuki." Qhasheik whistled and put his hands on his hips. "You look like the poster girl for a bondage-porn movie. I like." He nudged Abiditan.

Abiditan ignored his companion's observation. "*Naelf*, you don't have to do this, you know." He tilted his head toward Qhasheik standing next to him. "You know we can just head back to the Nergal with no one the wiser."

Before they left the ship orbiting the planet, Qhasheik had injected them with automatic transfer beacons in their inner wrists that would activate once pushed. "Don't worry about Murduk in stasis. Before we leave the solar system, we'll jettison the ass out an airlock like Qhasheik suggested."

He held his fist out for Qhasheik's bump.

"Got that right, bro." Qhasheik licked his lips and leered at Katsuki. "You don't even have to change or anything. That outfit is giving me all kinds of ideas for once we hit our private chambers."

"Can't you think of anything besides sex?" Katsuki groused as she bent over to pick up her flat shoes to put on.

With the globes of her ass in the air, Abiditan's higher reasoning went south. Fuck. Q had a point about what their female wore.

"No."

Katsuki straightened with a sigh. "Look. I get why you think this is a bad idea. But would either one of you do anything different if it was your family's legacy on the line? I can't let Eiael get away with stealing my home. No telling what she's done to Narkata since I've been gone."

She glanced around the small chamber as if to make sure nobody heard what she said next.

Not that they could fit anybody else in the small closet of a room they'd put them in for her to get ready. He couldn't believe how quickly the challenge was going to happen. Not even a full day passed since Katsuki demanded the *ya-ya... yang... yung*, whatever that damn thing was called in the first place.

"And I think there's something bigger going on here. No way would Queen Arelle hide in her rooms if someone kidnapped her daughter. And to let Prince Aylzrunth off planet with no support?" She snorted and shook her head. "No way. That bitch Horisa has to be in league with someone on the Judicial Council trying to wrestle power away from the monarchy. This is the first step in putting things right."

Shit. Her flat, steadfast tone told him that nothing he or Qhasheik said would change it.

"I don't know why you're so worried." She sat on a chair and slipped the leather shoes on her feet. "Eiael has always been a lazy moocher who never worked a day in her life. Whereas the three of us have practiced Muay Thai kickboxing for years." She stood with a triumphant grin. "Stupid *hysta* doesn't stand a chance. I'll have her flat on her ass and out like that," she snapped her fingers. "Wait and see. I'll do it within the first five seconds too. And to make it sorta fair, I won't take in any weapons."

Abiditan groaned. "Katsuki."

Qhasheik laughed. "*Myressei!* You are a treasure."

Then the jerk enfolded their female in his arms. Trust him to take her side. Asshole.

Her pupilless neon-teal eyes focused on him. She held out a hand. "Come on, Abiditan. Give me a kiss before I take care of this little problem."

Damn Goddess Ninti! He took her hand and joined the group hug. The only thing left to do was pray they wouldn't regret this stupid idea.

Katsuki squinted when she went from the white Runihura sun into the closed arena where she was to battle for her family's honor.

The humongous darkened amphitheater was lit by long lights shadowed with lemon yellow and vivid teal, the colors of her House. Iridescent tubes ran under the bleachers and illuminated along the support beams that funneled upward. Inside, the main fighting arena was on a separate round dais that rose above the ground.

That way, everyone seated in the chamber had a good view of the battle. Strategically placed, massive video monitors hung above the seats, giving everyone a larger-than-life view of the match.

It was standing room only in the stadium. While the majority in the audience were females, most had brought the males of their households with them.

Warmth filled her as she glanced around at the audience. As she viewed the colorful blend of Runihura skin tones, something settled low inside. To be surrounded by the winter-white complexions from the House of Aryennes, to the hues of brick red from Kataperis, to the varying degrees of onyx black of the House of Aithalothes, to her own House with their bright-yellow skin tones. Taking a deep breath, she inhaled the familiar fragrances of her homeland. The spicy tang of the grilled meat of delicate horned *inugamis* along with the mouthwatering scent of baked goods from her childhood long forgotten. Her chest tightened. With renewed vigor, she promised the Lady of All Life to do her damnedest to win back the title of High Aspect of her House.

"Fellow citizens of Runihura!" The headshot of Magistrate Treva appeared on the hovering vids around the stadium. Her brick-red cheeks flushed a darker hue under the blistering yellow of her eyes. "A challenge has been claimed and accepted by the Judicial Council for the privilege of High Aspect for the house of Enochres."

Screams and catcalls mixed with whistles and boos. The crowd went wild.

Katsuki frowned. It seemed the populace was a bit more bloodthirsty than she remembered.

"I introduce to you, Katsuki Bargouda! The female we believed long dead has come back to life. She has demanded the Challenge of Yavanna against the current High Aspect ruling the planetoid Narkata, Eiael Pillick."

That was her cue. With head held high, Katsuki strolled out to the inner arena as if she didn't have a care in the world. Her close-up replaced Treva's on the screens.

The arena became still as indrawn breaths mingled with murmurs.

To give them a good show, she held out her arms until she reached the middle of the platform. Turning around in a circle, she let them get a good look at her.

All at once, thousands of Runihurans burst into thunderous applause and wild laughter.

A part of her had worried she'd been gone so long no one would remember her. Looked like she had nothing to worry about. She had risen from the dead, becoming the underdog. A symbol of hope. She stopped moving and placed her fists on her hips, waiting for her duplicitous cousin to appear.

She didn't have to wait long.

Instead of walking in on her own two feet, Eiael sat on an ornate chair just shy of being an opulent throne. Instead of wheels or hover capabilities, her chair sat aloft on the shoulders of four burly males clothed in nothing but slender loincloths.

Each one was a prime specimen from the ruling houses of Runihura. With a gentleness that belied their bulk, they set the chair down just outside of the walkway for Eiael to enter the combative ring.

Eiael struggled to pull her considerable body out of the tight seat. She would've fallen on her face if two of her males hadn't caught her by her arms. When she straightened, she yanked out of their grasp with a scowl. As if her stumble was their fault. She was the clumsy buffoon who didn't know how to work her own bulbous body.

With stoic expressions, they backed away from her with clenched fists at their sides.

Katsuki's opponent took her time walking down the pathway to the center. Along the way, she gave a regal nod here and there with a raised limp-wristed wave to the tepid reception of the audience.

Polite clapping was in direct contrast to the loud roar Katsuki had enjoyed.

She looked over her shoulder at Abiditan and Qhasheik, bound between two guards on the sidelines.

Abiditan grinned while Qhasheik's black eyebrows rose above wide eyes at the spectators' lukewarm response. His black lips pursed as if he whistled.

Not that she heard it this far away. She gave them a quick shrug and turned back to face Eiael.

For the first time, Katsuki noticed what the woman wore. She wrinkled her nose.

Eiael might be a substantial woman, but there was no reason for her to wear something that resembled a worker's overall two sizes too big. The pattern was a horrid jumble of mismatched images of squares, loops, and dots in a variety of silver tones that clashed with the brilliant-yellow tone of her skin. She wore thick gloves in gray that matched the clunky platform boots that reached up to her knees. Her beige-brown tresses were tucked under a tight aluminum-gray scarf.

Damn, Katsuki'd seen nothing so ugly in her life. The outfit made her unattractive relative downright homely.

"The rules of this combat are simple." Treva's headshot was prominent again on the floating monitors. "There are no champions allowed. While this is not a death challenge, in order for the champion to be announced, first blood has to be drawn. Each opponent may only take in what she has on, which doesn't include any blasters or similar devices. Once we announce the winner, the loser forfeits all rights and privileges to the house of Enochres. They will suffer banishment from Runihura and all its territories, including the moon Narkata. Also, all personal and legal possessions, including any mates or slaves, we will auction off to the highest bidder."

A brief picture of Abiditan and Qhasheik standing on the sidelines flashed on the vids.

Their handsome images created whoops and whistles of appreciation from the female population.

Katsuki narrowed her eyes at Magistrate Fehlel, who sat back with a possessive sneer on her thin white lips as she stared at Katsuki's men. *Keep looking, bitch. You'll never get my* aruus.

Both swore they'd activate their transmitter devices if she lost the match.

First chance she got, she'd do the same and meet them aboard the Nergal. Then they'd hightail it out of solar system of her homeworld before anyone knew what happened.

They'd figure out what to do with Murduk later.

"What weapon have you brought to this challenge, Eiael?"

With a gleeful smirk, Eiael slid a long cylindrical pole out of her loose sleeve.

Katsuki sucked in a breath.

It was a Stinger Whip, her cousin's favorite "toy" that she called "The Justifier".

The damn thing was made of industrial *gypgorite* steel that allowed several blows to be made within a matter of seconds. Back when they were in the training ring as preteens, Katsuki suffered one lash from the whip's bulbous tips. That "light" tap sliced through to the bone.

Eiael got punished by the adults back then for bringing such a dangerous weapon to a training session, and it took months for Katsuki's arm to heal. Her forearm still bore scars where the whip laid her skin bare. A slight shiver raced down her spine. She'd better take her cousin out quicker than she'd anticipated if she was going to come out unscathed.

"And you, Katsuki."

Treva's voice broke through her musings.

"What weapon do you bring to the ring?"

Katsuki didn't take her eyes off her opponent when she raised her arms to her side, palms up. "As you can see, Judicial Council, I only bring that which you see."

Eiael narrowed her eyes with a malicious sneer.

Katsuki's lifelong nemesis had to be up to something. She studied the loose, hideous outfit closer as a knot tightened in her belly. *Expect that which is not seen when in the presence of an unworthy adversary.* One of her favorite quotes from the Book of Creation as scribed by the Goddess Ninti. Right. No way would her rival enter the ring without cheating somehow.

Didn't matter. Sparring with Qhasheik and Abiditan over the years had taught her to never take anything for granted. Good thing it never entered their minds to hold back because she was a female.

Katsuki crouched. Holding one hand high behind her, she put the other in front of her. Rolling her wrist, she gave a clipped wave of her fingers that would have made Neo proud. Bring it. She was ready.

All around the amphitheater, the crowd lost their shit. Wild screams mixed with stomping feet and tumultuous applause.

"Are the combatants ready?"

Eiael sneered when she raised two fingers to indicate she was ready.

Katsuki gave her cousin an even stare when she raised two fingers as well.

"Combatants, do not engage until I give you the signal."

A shimmering force field encircled the two of them.

The sound of Treva's voice, along with the crowd, faded into the background. There, a hint of fear crossed Eiael's muddy orange eyes.

"Begin!"

Those orange eyes narrowed and the zing of The Justifier rang in the air.

Katsuki stepped forward and stuck her hand up, causing the strands of the whip to wrap around her wrist. The leather forearm guards she wore helped to minimize the pain the electrified barbs caused. She pulled with enough force that the whip flew out of Eiael's grip. Katsuki now had possession of the deadly weapon.

With a roar of rage, Eiael rushed at Katsuki, hitting her hard enough to make the whip fly and land several feet away.

The brawl began.

Eiael'd gained substantial weight over the years, and she used it to her best advantage.

Each grip by the woman crushed with an unnatural force. Those damn gloves had to have some kind of kinetic force embedded in them, giving Eiael added strength. Burrowing her arms in between, Katsuki snapped the woman's hold on her shoulders and thrust her opponent's hands off. She lodged one leg under her cousin and delivered several kicks.

They ended up in a fierce fight, using their elbows, open hands, and fists.

In a surprise move, Eiael put her hands around Katsuki's waist and flipped her onto her back. The hard impact to the ground made Katsuki lose her breath as stars clouded her vision.

Eiael straddled her substantial weight on Katsuki's stomach and grabbed her hands in a tight hold over her head. Leaning close to Katsuki's ear, she whispered. "If you think I'm going to ask you to yield, you'd be wrong. The only thing you're going to do is die."

With a villainous laugh straight out of some horrible Earth B-Movie, Eiael kept Katsuki's wrists in a firm grip with one hand while she let go with the other.

Out of the corner of her eye, Katsuki watched Eiael flex her gloved fingers. There, in the low light, the glint of embedded metal was clear to see.

"See that?"

The insidious smirk on her cousin's homely face was accompanied by a malicious giggle.

"I tipped these babies with the poison from a *sinlie*."

The glint of the sharp metal held Katsuki spellbound.

The *sinlie* was comparable to an Earth spider. That is, if the spider was the size of a small terrier from Earth.

One swipe from one of those needles would immobilize her. Each organ in her body would shut down, and she'd feel every ounce of agony.

"I'm going to enjoy watching you suffer before you die. Which you should have done so long ago when I had your ship sabotaged. I don't know how you and your disgusting daughter lived through that. You both should've suffered in that expanse of space, with no one near enough to rescue you. I can't tell you how many times I fantasized how the both of you died of hunger, or thirst, or froze in the vast coldness of space."

She leaned close until her fetid breath made it hard to breathe.

"Let's fix that mistake right now, hmm?" Eiael's gloved hand loomed close.

Katsuki tensed as heat flushed through her. Holding on to her temper by a mere thread, she instead let an evil leer of her own slide free. Too bad the stupid *sahu* sitting on top of her didn't realize Katsuki had her right where she wanted her. Now she had more than enough evidence to prove Eiael tried to cheat in the sacred Yavanna challenge. "Not today, bitch."

She looped her dominant leg around one of Eiael's and used her opposite knee to push the woman off, and then rolled on top of her. Grabbing The Justifier that was now within reach, she wrapped the metal thongs of the whip around her cousin's throat and pulled tight.

Eiael kicked and squirmed, grabbing Katsuki's wrists around the leather armbands, which were more than enough protection against the sharp needles.

Watching the traitor's eyes bug out and her yellow face turn orange settled the raging fury coursing through Katsuki. A sense of calm took over. Now she could finish this the right way. She loosened the hold of The Justifier around Eiael's neck so the woman could breathe. Taking the end of one thong of the whip, she scraped it against the woman's chin.

Silver blood bubbled and rolled free.

She jumped off her opponent and stepped back, arms raised, with a yell of victory.

"First blood is drawn!" Treva's voice rang loud and true. "The challenge of Yavanna is complete. Katsuki Bargouda has regained all rights and privileges as a citizen of Runihura, and the title of High Aspect for the House of Enochres is hers!"

Screams, screeches, and catcalls met with foot stomping, along with whistles from the stadium audience.

Standing proudly next to her now-subdued cousin, she addressed the podium where the Judicial Council sat. "Magistrates, I have proof that Eiael Pillick not only tried to cheat during the sacred rights of Yavanna, I have, by her own words, proof that she tried to kill me and my daughter." The camera vid she'd embedded on the leather choker around her neck recorded everything her cousin said and tried to do.

Damn, it was good to be alive.

CHAPTER TWELVE

Ah, was there anything better than being in the middle of a pod sandwich? If there was, Katsuki couldn't think of it. Abiditan kissed her as if desperate to absorb her to him, while Qhasheik enfolded them both in his massive arms, his chest flush against her back, his hard-as-iron cock poking her lower back. She tilted her head to give him more room to suckle the skin between her neck and shoulder.

The small dressing room they were in after the match didn't provide enough space to move around in.

Abiditan broke the kiss and nuzzled the front of her neck. "Let's go someplace where we can do the things I have in mind."

He peppered each word with a light nibble that made her skin pebble.

"Screw that." Qhasheik burrowed his hands under the bra device and squeezed the mounds of her breasts, pinching her nipples.

She gasped as tendrils of lust shot to her core.

"This cramped place will do just fine. Everyone else can all freakin' go to hell. Lock the door behind you, Abiditan." One of his clever hands left her breasts and traveled down her stomach until reaching the thong covering her sex, tunneling under the fabric.

She stood on tiptoe, trying to help him reach his goal. She purred and looped her arms behind her to wrap around his neck.

"High Aspect Bargouda? Are you in there?" A stern female voice yelled while something pounded on the door. "Magistrate Islebell demands your appearance at once. High Aspect?"

"This fucking planet is getting on my last damn nerve." Qhasheik growled. "Hey, person buggin' the shit outta us. Look down the hall. You know what I see?" His rough voice was loud enough to be heard through the closed door. "It's you going away!"

There was a brief hesitation before the pounding on the door resumed. "High Aspect? Magistrate Islebell insists you join her at her private office at once. And no one keeps Magistrate Islebell waiting."

"Tell the Magistrate that impatience can cause wise people to do stupid things!" Abiditan shouted at the closed door. He reached behind Qhasheik, grabbing the globes of his ass, causing all three of their groins to rub against each other. He sucked in a breath and closed his mismatched eyes.

"The Magistrates do not have time to be impatient." Another booming bang on the door.

It took a moment before what the unknown woman said hit Katsuki. Her bark of laughter defused the sensual web holding her spellbound. "All right, guys. Let's take care of this last bit of nonsense, then we'll go home to Narkata." She gave Abiditan a quick kiss. "I promise, we'll have plenty of space there." She turned to give Qhasheik his kiss.

"I don't suppose you'll go just like that?" Qhasheik indicated the minuscule battle clothes she had on. He put a strand of his black hair behind his ear, showing off his dilated pupils that left his red irises in a thin ring when he gazed at her chest.

She scrunched her nose. "Huh?"

"While Qhasheik and I wouldn't mind you flashing these beauties around," Abiditan pulled the bra top away from her chest and reached in to place her breasts inside. "We'd rather you didn't have these treasures out for others to ogle."

Damn males. All they had to do was touch her, and she'd throw caution to the winds to indulge in some much-needed sensual play. Well, crap. Sucking in a grown-up breath, she tamped the urge to let loose and say the hell with everything else.

"Inform the Magistrate I'll be there as soon as I change." She raised her voice and spoke over her shoulder at the closed door. To her pod mates, she held up a finger to keep them from arguing with her. "I'm going to the refresher to get cleaned up before I put on some decent clothes." She gave them both a narrow-eyed glare. "Alone."

With their arms crossed, they stood with wide stances and glared back.

She smiled at their identical pouts. They were so adorable.

Using one of the coliseum's various Transkip mirrors, Katsuki and her men followed the female guard to the reception room at the judicial chambers. It surprised her there wasn't a contingent of guards walking with them in public. How odd the Council felt comfortable enough to let her and her men wander through the sacred chambers without more guards to monitor them. She looked over her shoulder at the humongous woman behind them. But then again, they didn't need a contingent of soldiers when they had her.

She doubted this female needed others to help her guard anything or anyone. Even without body armor. The woman had to be one of the most massive females she'd ever seen. Her chest was wide enough that two Katsukis could've stood side-by-side and still had room. As far as she could tell, there wasn't an ounce of fat on the female.

Her freakin' muscles had muscles, showcased by the simple, sleeveless black shirt tucked into formfitting dark-purple leather pants. Seamless mid-calf clunky black boots were thick enough to protect her feet. On each hip was a holster that held two blasters and several recharging cartridges. Strapped across her broad back was a laser spear. Knives nestled in tight pouches around her thighs. With each step, the handles of the deadly weapons glinted in the light. You'd think there was a war on, given how heavily armored the woman was.

The female's porcelain-white skin and amethyst eyes proclaimed her to be from the house of Aryennis. She'd shaved her purple hair into a buzz cut, exposing a deep scar that bisected the right side of her head and slashed across her thin lips, ending at the corner of her chin.

Katsuki didn't doubt her own fighting abilities, but getting into the ring with this one would stretch her skills to the limit. Thank The Lady of All Life, Eiael couldn't bring in a champion. No doubt the outcome might've ended up a little differently.

Instead of showing them into the formal council chamber, the woman led them to an office marked "private".

Crossing the threshold, they entered a glass atrium that blended into the building architecture. The round, glass roof created an open-space sensation, giving the illusion they were outdoors. The various plants and flowers created a soothing scent of floral calm.

Katsuki inhaled the long-forgotten comforting aromas of her home planet.

In the middle of the room was a floating water fountain that didn't appear to sit on any base. Cool, purple liquid bubbled in a soothing melody.

Next to the flowing water sat Magistrate Islebell in a hover chair nestled close to an oblong table made of precious wood from a nearby forest. With calm precision, she poured hot, clear-pink liquid into four cups. "Please sit. Relax and enjoy some River Petal tea with me. I'm sure you are quite famished after that challenge." She nodded to the behemoth female. "Thank you, Brunna. You may leave."

"Are you sure, Magistrate?" Brunna scowled at Abiditan and Qhasheik. The twist of her thin lips made the puckered skin of her scar stretch her mouth into an unnatural sneer. "These males don't look trustworthy."

Islebell nodded with a reassuring smile. "I'm sure. Please stand watch outside the closed door. I'll call you if I need you."

Brunna curled her upper lip as her shiny amethyst eyes glared. "Yes, Magistrate."

Katsuki breathed a sigh of relief when the female left. It had been a toss-up on who would lose their patience with the guard first. Either Abiditan would address the aggressive female with his best aristocratic put-down or Qhasheik would unleash his smart-ass tongue. Or worse, they'd do it together.

"Katsuki."

Islebell waved to a plush, levitating seat next to her. "Come sit." She turned and looked at Abiditan and Qhasheik. Glancing back at Katsuki who had seated herself, she leaned in to whisper with a girlish grin. "Are you sure you don't want to place them on the block as well?"

The magistrate licked her lips and flickered a look at Katsuki's men again. "I would be more than willing to take them off your hands with an extremely generous offer. I assure you, I will treat them with the utmost respect."

The hiss of the men's indrawn breaths behind them made Katsuki realize she'd never explained the caste system on Runihura. Dammit, first chance she'd relay how they treated "slaves" on Runihura.

Instead of the abuse and neglect that happened on Akurn, it was the complete opposite here. Most of those who put themselves up for auction came from poor families looking for a chance at training or a permanent employment. Each case differed, depending on what kind of training or employment was involved. While most them became indentured for a couple of years, others agreed to a lifelong appointment. Runihura law dealt in the harshest manner with any citizen who abused or neglected their indentured servants.

Katsuki gave her men a teasing, wide smile over her shoulder.

They frowned in response. Abiditan's mismatched eyes of sea green and translucent, dove gray narrowed in warning.

With a dramatic sigh, she shook her head and faced her distant cousin. "These men aren't my slaves." Well, not counting what happened in the bedroom. "They are my eternal soulmates, my *aruus*. I'll never part from them." She took both their hands as they stood behind her chair. She gripped them tight, keeping their warmth against her collarbone.

They squeezed back in response.

"Ever." They'd face whatever happened to Narkata together.

"Well—" Islebell shrugged. "—if you're sure." She gestured to the opposite side of the table. "Males, please have a seat and enjoy some tea." She indicated the steaming cups beside her. With a steady hand, she set the half-full carafe on the table before lifting her delicate cup to her lips. She took a tiny sip before putting the cup down, keeping her fingers around it.

Once Abiditan and Qhasheik sat, she continued. "I understand you brought with you a convicted felon, as declared by the Federation Consortium, for Runihura justice." She sat back. "I have read the report of his crimes that you brought back with you from Akurn. I must say, I agree death would be too good for him. Since he has committed hideous crimes against someone in our House, it's up to me as the judicial head of Enochres to decide his fate. If you would be so kind as to bring him here, we'll have this taken care of right away." She waved to the glass wall behind her made of mirrors. "You're more than welcome to use my Transkip."

"Nah." Qhasheik jumped up. "I'll be right back." After a sharp salute, he pushed the transportation button embedded in his wrist and disappeared.

Islebell's cinnamon-brown eyebrows rose. "Why wouldn't he use the Transkip to retrieve your prisoner?"

"Because he's a freaking show-off." Abiditan grumbled.

Before she responded, Qhasheik came through the Transkip with the stasis pod holding Murduk hovering next to him. "Where do ya want him?"

Islebell went over and examined the face of the prisoner embedded inside the stasis pod. She pursed her lips. "Too bad. He's such a handsome brute." Without looking behind her, she shouted. "Brunna!"

The beastly Brunna rushed into the room, clutching a blaster and pointing it between Qhasheik and Abiditan. "Which one should I shoot first?"

Katsuki and Islebell laughed.

Damn, this monstrosity of a woman sure was predictable.

"Stand down, Brunna. I want you to take this male out of stasis." She pointed to the coffin-shaped stasis pod. "Put a *katr* over his mouth before you release him. I have no desire to listen to anything he has to say." She resumed her seat at the table. Picking up her teacup, she took another delicate sip. "You may inform Good Elder Irkalla of the house of Kataperis that her new companion is here and is ready for her to claim."

With a deep grunt, Brunna shoved her blaster into the holster on her hip. Scowling, she held out her hand for Qhasheik to give her the remote control of the hovering pod.

With a grimace, Qhasheik dropped it into her hand.

Katsuki grinned at his disgusted expression.

The gargantuan female turned to the pod and began the sequence to release Murduk from his enforced deep sleep.

With a self-satisfied smile, Islebell leaned close to whisper to Katsuki. "As a welcome-home gift, I've provided a special treat for you regarding this male's fate." Her aquamarine eyes twinkled.

"Really?" Katsuki glanced at her men.

After giving Brunna the remote, Qhasheik sat next to her with eyebrows raised. Abiditan sat next to him and pursed his lips.

She regarded Islebell again. "What...?"

All heads turned to the door when it whooshed open.

"Ah, here she is. Right on time."

With a fluid grace Katsuki envied, Islebell left the table and joined a wizened elderly female who shuffled in, leaning most of her slight weight on a thick wooden cane with intricate carvings.

Islebell leaned towards the elderly female and grabbed her gnarled hand with a pat. "I am so glad you could come on such short notice, Elder Irkalla." Her tone was soft with respect.

The tiny elder's head reached just below Islebell's shoulders. The dark, brick red of her face was mottled with black age spots, but her brilliant-white eyes were clear. "Yes, yes. Take me to this upstart so that I may determine his punishment."

"What the fuck?" Qhasheik side-whispered to Katsuki. "You're going to hand over dickwad to this little old lady?"

Abiditan sucked in a sharp breath. "Katsuki, you can't think this is a good idea." He pushed his chair away as if to stand.

She placed a hand on his forearm to stop him.

With a frown, he sat without taking his gaze off Islebell and the elderly woman.

"Don't worry. Let's just see what Magistrate Islebell has planned." From her seat, Katsuki watched Islebell escorting the waddling efforts of Elder Irkalla as they reached the now-freed Murduk. A bound-and-gagged Murduk. She sat back and studied the disgraced Akurn.

Before putting him in stasis, the Royals only allowed him to be dressed in tight, navy-blue Speedos, leaving the rest of him bare to showcase Murduk's ghost-white skin in all its glory. Hanging limp in front of him, his hands were in binding cuffs made of *gypgorite* steel, the hardest known substance in the galaxy. His platinum hair hung in greasy strands to his shoulders.

If she wasn't mistaken, he appeared to have lost some tone and definition in his frame during his captivity. She stared at the grayish tint on his skin as his stare darted around him. It always bothered her the color of Murduk's eyes resembled hers. She only hoped her turquoise eyes never had the cold, deadly glint his glare carried.

"As you can see, Elder Irkalla, he is a hale-and-hearty male. Nary a mark or blemish." Islebell turned to the pair of male servants who'd accompanied Irkalla. "Get the Good Elder a seat."

The servants scrambled and rushed out of the room and soon returned with a hover chair.

Holding onto the elderly woman's arm, Islebell helped her to sit when they placed it behind her.

The chair transformed around the woman into a plush seat.

"Yes, yes. No need to fuss." Elder Irkalla waved everyone away.

Her attendants bowed and stepped back, but didn't go far.

"Now, show him to me." She tapped her cane on the floor.

"Brunna." Islebell nodded to the behemoth woman.

With a stiff grin, Brunna pressed a button to activate the *Nutesh* snare around Murduk's neck.

It forced him to walk forward until she clicked it to make him stop a few feet from where Irkalla sat.

Katsuki pressed her lips together to stop from laughing.

Murduk's forehead beaded with sweat as his face flushed.

Heh, too bad the bastard was now compelled to live a life he didn't want. Served him right for all the time he made others live as oppressed slaves, forced to do his bidding.

"He's a scrawny, ugly thing, isn't he?" Elder Irkalla sat back. She glanced at Islebell standing next to her. "Your offer said he came "as is", correct?"

"Then we agree? You will purchase this male to serve you for the rest of his days?" A serene smile crossed Islebell's face.

"Yes, yes. I suppose he'll do for what I have in mind."

Katsuki gasped. "Magistrate, I don't think you understand what a dangerous individual he is."

Islebell patted Katsuki's hand with a reassuring nod. "Don't worry. Elder Irkalla and I have discussed all the modifications he'll need, regardless of where he ends up on Runihura."

"Modifications?" Abiditan leaned forward with his head cocked and a raised eyebrow.

"Why, we'll inject him with the Terminal Mutagen before we leave this room. Yes, yes." Elder Irkalla tapped her cane on the floor twice. "Better than any prison cell."

"What's that?" Qhasheik sat back and crossed an ankle over a knee, drumming his fingers on the tabletop.

Magistrate Islebell resumed her seat. "It's a biological poison that acts as a tracker. Once it's injected into the bloodstream, there's no way to take it out. It becomes a part of his DNA."

"But how will that prevent him from escaping?" Abiditan frowned.

"Well, for one there's no way to turn the tracker off. If he ever strays from the perimeters we've installed in its genome, it'll alert his handlers. Who can activate the lurking poison any time, or it will automatically deploy if he leaves Runihura. He'd suffer a painful death as each organ in his body broke down and liquefied." Islebell took another sip of her cooling tea. "He'd end up dead before he left our atmosphere." She set her teacup down and faced the gargantuan woman. "Brunna, if you'd be so kind." She motioned to a side table across the room. "Please inject him now."

"At once, Magistrate." Brunna spun on her heels to grab a blue cylinder tube. Without a word, she faced Murduk and pushed his head aside, pressing the tube against his neck.

His breathing accelerated as his wide eyes darted as if seeking help. He winced when the broad woman pressed the end, creating a slight hiss.

"Yes, yes. That's done." Elder Irkalla struggled to stand, gripping the top of her cane for support.

Her male servants rushed over to help her.

"I'm fine. I'm fine. We must get going. Mustn't be late for the appointment at the Royal clinic. My babies must be desperate since I've been gone so long." She started shuffling out of the room, her two servants walking close to her with their arms raised, as if to catch her if she fell.

Katsuki swore she'd come into the middle of a movie and hadn't watched the beginning of the story. She walked over to Elder Irkalla, grasping the woman with a light touch to turn and face her. "I don't understand. What do you want him for, and why are you going to the Royal clinic?"

Elder Irkalla paused and rested with both her hands gripping the top of the cane. "Why, I need somebody to shepherd my precious Omopards! I have the largest ranch in Runihura that breeds and sells them. My prize-winning darlings are the choice of any House wishing to purchase them. I assure you, the demand for them is quite high." She glanced behind her and nodded to the servant following. "Buzby, activate that male's collar and bring him with us. We can't be late for our appointment."

Brunna handed the remote to the younger brick-red male.

He clicked the gadget and forced Murduk to walk with them.

Katsuki watched the elder's humped figure continue her journey out of the room. "But why are you taking him to the clinic?" She asked the woman's retreating back.

"Like any other conscientious owner of a domesticated animal, I need to make sure he's up to date on all his shots before he's neutered!" Without another word, the matron and her servants, along with an unresisting Murduk, left the room.

Katsuki's jaw dropped as she stared at the closed door. A roar of twin male guffaws, along with a slap on the table, sounded behind her. With a bemused smile, she met them back at the table.

Magistrate Islebell poured herself another cup of tea.

"Holy shit, Katsuki!" Qhasheik snickered. "That's the best freakin' thing I've ever heard."

"Yeah," Abiditan retorted. "But what's an Omopard? Some kind of cow or something?"

"Shit, I hope not." Qhasheik sat up. "Being a cowboy would be way too romantic for that asshole."

"Let me show you." Islebell motioned for one of her servants by the door. "Would you let Dede Divine in, please?"

Katsuki couldn't wait to the see the looks on her men's faces when Islebell's pet came in. While she'd never indulged in owning one of the rare, prized animals, she knew plenty of people who did.

An animal the size of an Earth fox—with six legs and a thick, fuzzy tail—strutted through the door. Long, fluffy, pale-pink fur covered its delicate skin while its navy-blue ears were pointed like a fox's. The creature strolled to Islebell and rubbed against her ankles with a loud purr that was part dog growl and part cat rumble.

Islebell didn't hesitate to pick the creature up to place it on her lap. She stroked between the creature's ears and scratched under the jewel-encased collar around its neck.

Katsuki had never noticed before how this domesticated animal's wide pupilless gray eyes reminded her of an owl. Or an anime character.

The Omopard raised up on its hind legs and tried to get close to Islebell's cup of tea. With a flick of its midnight-blue forked tongue, it leaned in, trying to take a sip of the pink liquid.

She peeked at Qhasheik and Abiditan and snickered.

Both had identical expressions of mixed horror, their mouths and eyes wide open.

"No, Dede." Islebell tapped her pet's snout. "Remember what happened last time you did that? You were sick for a week."

"That's what Murduk has to herd?" Disbelief laced Abiditan's voice. "I think he'd rather be dead."

"Ha! Suck me sideways!" Qhasheik slapped his knee with a hoot. "I can't wait to tell everyone Murduk ended up a eunuch cat wrestler!"

EPILOGUE

Katsuki directed Qhasheik to the landing strip where the spaceship Nergal could be placed. Used for generations, the pad was next to the main house, the Fydaesia Citadel. As she walked down the gangplank with her men, her eyes widened and she halted and stood with her arms crossed.

Instead of the expected pristine landing area, signs of neglect were everywhere. The main control building on her right was falling apart. Broken and missing windows, ragged holes in the walls, and a caved-in roof. The ground was covered in potholes so extensive, she doubted any land vehicle could use it. How that happened was a mystery. That repudiated the strip being indestructible since it was made of *gypgorite* steel, the main alloy mined on Narkata.

All around, the supporting structures had pieces missing, as if thieves had stripped them.

And where was everyone? As the lifeblood of the mining operation, there should've been servants or freemen bustling around, performing the various tasks to keep the airfield in top condition. Without this airfield up and running, there was no way to get the ore to Runihura for processing.

Qhasheik stopped beside her and put her arm around her shoulder. "No offense, *myressei*, but I've seen better."

Abiditan snorted. "Let's hope the main house doesn't look like this."

Katsuki pressed a fist against her chest. She swore her heart shrunk. "I knew Eiael was a lazy bitch, but I can't believe she'd let things get this far."

"Maybe we should use the Transkip in the ship. I doubt there's a working one out here." He squeezed her neck and kissed her temple before letting go. He put his hands on his hips and looked around.

Katsuki pointed to one of the dilapidated buildings. "Yeah, there used to be a Transkip over there, but I doubt it's up and running with the roof caved in like that." With a bitter smile, she motioned her men to follow her. "Without knowing the state of the main house, I think it'd be safer to walk there instead. Come on. A little exercise never hurt anyone." She patted Qhasheik's flat stomach. "Even you, big boy."

"Yeah, well, I'd rather use my energy for something way more productive." He gave Katsuki a suggestive leer.

Abiditan smacked the back of Qhasheik's head. "Get your mind out of the gutter, dhasa. Can't you see she's upset?"

Qhasheik rubbed the back of his head. His extra limb between his horns twitched at the slight abuse. He glared. "Ow, dude. No need for hostilities." He then nudged his pod partner with an elbow and a wide grin. "You know you were thinking the same thing. You're just too chicken to say it out loud."

Used to their playful banter, Katsuki headed toward the main house. Glancing around the dusty environment, she was glad she'd changed clothes aboard the Nergal. She wore one of her favorite suits that had a sleek, pinstriped, indigo vest with a deep v-line in front that held up her heavy breasts. Over the vest was a jacket in the same pattern she had tailor-made by a seamstress on Azadi who specialized in Earth attire. Short in the front at her waist with tails longer on the back. The breathable material gave her plenty of room to move around. She'd tucked the matching formfitting pants into knee-high boots, complete with sensible heels.

She stiffened her shoulders as a profusion of nerves made her grimace. Might as well see the rest of the place. Good thing she'd included various weapons in and under the suit. Given the state of neglect all around her, no telling what might happen.

To reach the Citadel, they had to pass through a small village, Enochres Hallow, where the miners and their families lived.

The eerie silence as they walked through the run-down buildings made her eyes water. Looping an arm through Abiditan's elbow, she leaned on him for support.

"What happened here? Did everyone leave?" She gazed around, trying to find signs of life.

But most of the buildings were boarded up or had missing doors and empty windows. The town square used to be vibrant, with charming exotic plants lining the walkways and perfuming the air. In the center of the village was one of their proudest additions. Like a huge water fountain on Earth, they'd installed a fountain of light boasting various shades of colors bubbling with tinkling music to soothe even the weariest patron.

It lay broken in half on the unforgiving dust, silent as death.

"Oh, they're still here." Qhasheik kept in step on her other side. "They're watching every move we make."

Katsuki grabbed his arm to make him stop and look at her. "People are still here? Are you sure?"

He patted her hand with a warm smile. "Of course I'm sure." He twirled his dark finger. "They're all over the place. Seems like hiding has become an art form here."

"Well, shit." Katsuki let go of Qhasheik and headed to the broken-down light fountain. She stood on a part of the remaining basin and faced what she hoped was the direction where people could see her.

"Good people of Enochres Hallow. You may not remember me, but I am High Aspect Katsuki Bargouda, the head of the House of Enochres." She spread her arms wide. "I'm sorry I've been gone so long that you have suffered in my absence."

"And just where have you been, High Aspect?"

A tall, regal female walked from behind one of the crumbling buildings. By her bright-yellow skin tone, it was clear she was a member of Katsuki's House. A beige scarf matching the loose pants and blouse covered the woman's head. The caramelized orange of her eyes was narrow with distrust.

It took a moment before Katsuki recognized her as Ioxedae, the Castellan of Fydaesia Citadel.

As the woman spoke, several people came out of hiding, mumbling with angry tones.

"Ioxadae." Katsuki gestured to the crumbling and neglected village. "What happened here?"

"No, *High Aspect.*" Ioxade spat as she sneered the title, standing with her hands on her hips. "When you deserted us and left us at the mercy of that *lilit*, you lost any right to know anything about us."

Katsuki couldn't swallow past the lump in her throat as tears gathered. When she glanced at the crowd, it was easy to see starvation had taken its toll. The thin frames of her people were hard to take in.

Qhasheik and Abiditan stood on the ground next to her perch. Qhasheik reached over with a comforting hand and enclosed it around her thigh.

His touch gave her the surge of strength she sorely needed. "I'm so sorry to see what Eiael has done to you." She threw her shoulders back. "But I won the Challenge of Yavanna against her and have regained control over the House of Enochres and all of Narkata."

Ioxedae crossed her arms. "Again, High Aspect, I ask. Where have you been?"

Katsuki stepped down from the base of the light fountain and approached the other woman. "Just as my cousin betrayed you, she did the same to Arzea and me. Eiael sabotaged our spaceship to break down in the dead space between the pleasure planet of Agon and Runihura. The ship suffered a complete system breakdown, and we would've died if it weren't for the fact the rogue planet Akurn was near enough to "rescue" us."

There were gasps from the elders in the group.

The rogue planet Akurn was infamous for invading and conquering the various systems in the galaxy.

Ioxeada's expression softened. "I assume they enslaved you. How did you get away?" She peered at the men behind Katsuki. "And where is Lady Arzea? Did she not make it?"

The small crowd drew closer as if to offer support.

For the first time since the small group came out, hope blossomed. The mood of the people turned to one of sympathy rather than anger. She reached over and grasped Ioxeada's hands. "They separated us when we were first captured. I only recently discovered she still lives." She glanced at Abiditan with a mischievous smile. "Good thing my daughter was smart enough to hide in their sacred temple that only allowed females in. She studied and thrived there until she met and mated her *aruu*."

During their journey to Runihura, Katsuki and Arzea had a chance to get caught up. It thrilled her that her daughter not only found her *aruu* in Amil-Shamish, but would be soon be the proud mother of their son, Laneus-Zadtus, due any cycle now.

"Will she be joining us soon?" This question came from a younger member of their House.

The female's name escaped Katsuki, but she recognized her as one of Arzea's closest friends.

"I'm afraid not." Katsuki shook her head. "She and her mate are expecting their first child. So I doubt she'll be able to join us for quite some time." Not to mention her daughter was now Queen Consort of Akurn, and leaving the planet during their time of turmoil wasn't likely to happen. But that was a tale for a later time.

Katsuki released her hold on Ioxeada's hands and glanced around the dilapidated village. "I'm so sorry you suffered because of my cousin's selfishness. But we're here now to set things right." She couldn't swallow with a dry mouth. "Please tell me, what does Fydaesia Citadel look like?"

Ioxeada's shoulders slumped. "High Aspect, Eiael banished us, and we weren't allowed anywhere near it for cycles. The only way we survived is because of our families and friends who remained there. From what we understand, most of the Citadel is falling into disrepair." She tilted her head and gave Katsuki a weak smile. "Except for those areas that she lived in. She upgraded them as much as she could and fell into a gluttonous, hedonistic lifestyle."

Damn bitch. Banishment wasn't good enough for the cow. "And what about the mine? Why don't I hear the machines working?" Without production, where was the money coming from?

"Mistress, if I may?" This from the female who stood at Ioxeada's side.

If Katsuki wasn't mistaken, that was Stega, who'd worked as the mining forewoman.

"While some of the mining equipment still works, the continual neglect of the key machinery made most of the production sporadic several cycles ago. It produces just enough ore to keep the Citadel running, with barely enough left over for the rest of us."

Qhasheik and Abiditan joined her on each side.

"How far is the Citadel from here?" Abiditan asked as he wrapped an arm around her waist.

Qhasheik put his palm on her shoulder with a gentle squeeze.

"We'll be able to see it just over that rise there." Katsuki pointed to a small hill at the edge of town. She trembled as her heart raced. She'd rather face a thousand foes in the challenge ring rather than see the horrendous shape her childhood home had to be in. Taking in a deep breath, she gave her man a wobbly smile. "Let's take a look, shall we?"

"Well, hell, I ain't got nothing else to do. Do you?" Qhasheik whistled as he led the way, as if he knew where he was going.

Abiditan shook his head. "One of these days, he's going to find himself somewhere he shouldn't be."

"Yeah," Katsuki agreed. "And we're just dumb enough to be right there with him."

Qhasheik stopped at the top of the hill and put his fists on his trim hips.

She couldn't help but sigh as she examined the neon-orange thigh-high shorts that showcased the wondrous globes of his firm ass.

As usual, he didn't wear a shirt, just unnecessary suspenders. Today they were lime green, a striking contrast against his eggplant-colored skin. His black, rounded, ram's horns glistened as he moved his head back and forth studying the surroundings.

When they joined Qhasheik at the top of the hill, Katsuki's heart dropped at her first look at Fydaesia Citadel.

The once-proud and majestic three-story building lay crumbling in the unforgiving sun. The inner support structure was *gypgorite* steel, but the outside boasted various adobe-and-stone paneling intended to give it a distinguished air. Now, most of the walls were falling apart, with broken windows prominent.

"Wow, what a du.... wonderful looking place!"

Katsuki didn't miss what Qhasheik almost said. With a sad smile, she had to agree. "Yeah, well getting this place back to its former glory was going to take a lot of work. Not to mention needed funds."

"Hey, no problem!" Abiditan fist-bumped his male pod mate on the shoulder. "All we gotta do is off

"Heh, we'd get more bank for you, boyo." Qhasheik smacked Abiditan on the back of his black T-shirt. "You're way prettier than I am."

"Quiet. Or I'll put you both on the block as a matched pair." Katsuki crossed her arms and studied the devasted landscape. On the outside, it looked hopeless, but where there was a will, there was potential.

"Okay, boys. Roll up your sleeves. We've got work to do."

A SMALL ASK...

Now that you've finished reading **Qhasheik's Pod,** it'd mean the world to me if you left an honest review wherever you bought it. This type of feedback is an authors lifeblood and helps others find their work. I can't continue writing sizzling adventures without you.

Thank you!

ABOUT THE AUTHOR

Keri Kruspe, award-winning *"Author of Otherworldly Romantic Adventures"* loves nothing more than to write about romances that feature "feisty heroines who are afraid to take a chance on life... or love". Her writing career started when she became irritate that most SciFi Alien Romances had women kidnapped before love found them. Determined to create something different, she turned "the alien kidnapping trope upside down" (Vine Voice) and the ***ALIEN EXCHANGE*** trilogy was born.

Keri's latest SciFi Romance series, ***ANCIENT ALIEN DESCENDATNS***, is taking the Ancient Alien motif and mixes it with a sensual, romantic twist.

A native Nevadan, Keri is a lifelong avid reader who lives in northwestern Michigan with her hubby and the newest member of the family, a Jack Russell Terrier names Hestia. When not immersed in her made-up worlds, she enjoys discovering the fascinating landscape of her new home and pairing red wine with healthy ways to cook. Most of all, she loves finding her next favorite author.

If you want to know when Keri's next book will come out, please visit her at her website where you can sign up for her mailing list. You'll get a
FREE copy of the novella, *The Day Behind Tomorrow* that is a prologue to the ***ANCIENT ALIEN DESCENDANT SERIES***. Not to mention being kept updated on the life of a dedicated, obsessed author.

Social Media Links:

Facebook

Twitter

Instagram

ALSO BY KERI

Alien Legacy: The Vampire

Alien Legacy: The Mage

<u>More Novellas Coming in 2003</u>

Claude & Amata

Lok's Love

<u>Alien Legacy Brotherhood</u>

Coming soon